THE
BREAD SISTER
⇥ OF ⇤
SINKING
CREEK

ROBIN MOORE

THE BREAD SISTER OF SINKING CREEK

HarperTrophy ®
A Division of HarperCollinsPublishers

The Bread Sister of Sinking Creek
Copyright © 1984 by Robin Moore
All rights reserved. No part of this book may be used or reproduced in any manner
whatsoever without written permission except in the case of brief quotations embodied
in critical articles and reviews. Printed in the United States of America. For information
address HarperCollins Children's Books, a division of HarperCollins Publishers,
10 East 53rd Street, New York, NY 10022.
Typography by Joyce Hopkins

Library of Congress Cataloging-in-Publication Data
Moore, Robin.
   The bread sister of Sinking Creek / by Robin Moore.
      p.   cm.
   Summary: Fourteen-year-old Maggie Callahan, who has a special talent for making
bread, struggles to survive on the Pennsylvania frontier in the late 1700s.
   ISBN 0-397-32418-9.—ISBN 0-397-32419-7 (lib. bdg.)
   ISBN 0-06-440357-2 (pbk.)
   [1. Orphans—Fiction.   2. Bread—Fiction.   3. Frontier and pioneer life—
Pennsylvania—Fiction.   4. Pennsylvania—Fiction.]   I. Title.
PZ7.M78766Br   1990   89-36400
[Fic]—dc20   CIP
                                                                                  AC

First HarperCollins edition, 1990.
First Harper Trophy edition, 1992.

This book is dedicated to three strong women:

My mother, Jeanne Catherine Moore,
Who filled my boyhood days with the smells of
fresh-baked bread.

My wife, Jacqueline Sonstein Moore,
Who believed in Maggie's story from the start and
kept the flame alive.

And my daughter, Rachel Sonstein Moore,
Who was born along with this book and has it all
ahead of her. . . .

I T WAS A HOT AFTERNOON, late in the summer of 1776, deep in the heart of the Pennsylvania wilderness. A hunched-over old man and a red-haired girl came riding single file up the mountain trail with a string of packhorses roped between them.

At the head of the packtrain rode Herbert Johnson, a mountain tinker who traveled from one wilderness community to another, peddling the trade goods carried on the backs of his pack animals. He was gnarled, old, and worn down like the mountains he rode through. Despite the heat, he wore a long overcoat, blackened and grease stained from a thousand campfires. His eyes were small and close together, like a possum's, and they peered out from under the wide brim of his hat, searching the trail ahead. His chin whiskers pointed the way up the mountainside.

Stepping along behind Mr. Johnson were his packhorses, heavily loaded now and roped together so they'd stay to the trail.

At the end of the packtrain rode Maggie Callahan. She was fourteen years old that summer. She was a fine-looking girl, with a touch of the Scotch-Irish in her features; the lines of her face were cut sure and clear, and her eyes were dark and direct. She wore her hair pulled back into a thick braid that trailed down the back of her dress, almost to her waist. The red of her hair picked up the sunlight and glowed like fire.

Like Herbert Johnson, she was filthy. Her ankle-length dress and the short blouse she wore over it were covered with dirt and stains. Her skirt had been snagged in so many places that she had given up mending it by the fire at night. She had an extra dress in her traveling sack, tied to the saddle horn, but she wanted to save that for a special occasion.

It surely was hot, Maggie thought. And quiet. She was amazed at how deathly still the forest could be on afternoons like this. The only sound was the monotonous creaking of the leather packsaddles and the labored breathing of the horses as they plodded up the mountain trail.

Maggie Callahan and Herbert Johnson were bound for Penn's Valley, which lay just north of the seven mountain ranges in the wild country of central Pennsylvania. The valley was so large and so impressive that on some of the old maps it was called simply "the Great Valley."

The Great Valley was where Maggie's new life lay. It was there that her Irish aunt Franny and her uncle Thomas had built themselves a homestead on forty acres of uncleared land. Here Maggie would make her new home.

Maggie had come nearly two hundred miles in the last fourteen days, and she was ready to leave the life of the trail behind her. More than that, she was ready to leave her whole past behind. She wanted the dark memories of Philadelphia to stay back on the other side of the Susquehanna River, where they belonged. For the first time in days, she was glad she had run away.

Maggie's thoughts flew ahead of them. Soon she would be sitting down to dinner with her aunt Franny's laughter and secrets, just as she had in the good days in Philadelphia. After all Maggie had been through, it would be good to be safe and secure and cared for for a while.

As the evening was coming on, Herbert Johnson

reined his horse to a stop and swung around in the saddle. He shouted back along the packtrain, loud enough for Maggie to hear, "There she be, Miz Callahan. The Great Valley."

Maggie nudged her horse and rode up to where Mr. Johnson sat. Through the mountain pass before them, Maggie saw a green and lovely valley, shadowed and peaceful in the evening light. This was the valley she had dreamed about for so long. It lay before them like a broad, flat map. Here and there she could see the curling plumes of chimney smoke rising from the individual homesteads. Somewhere down in the valley, she heard a dog barking. Far in the distance, another range of mountains, purple in the evening light, stretched across the horizon.

Johnson clucked to his horse and they rode down into the valley, to a place where several trails came together. The tinker halted the packtrain, swung down, and walked back to Maggie.

"Come down off the horse now, Miz Callahan."

Puzzled, Maggie obeyed.

Mr. Johnson began to work at the strings that held her traveling sack to the horn of the saddle.

"This here's the fork of the trail," he was saying. "That trail to the west—just a footpath, really—takes you up along the mountainside to where your aunt Franny's cabin sets. This other trail—this one to the north—heads out along the valley to General Potter's place. That's where I'm headed. Now you take the trail up along the mountainside and you'll be at your aunt Franny's door in less'n a mile."

"Now, wait a minute," Maggie said. "I thought you were going to take me there."

"Never said that," Mr. Johnson replied. "Said I'd bring you to the Great Valley. Here you be. Now I have business at Potter's tonight and you've slowed me down aplenty already."

He unlashed Maggie's traveling sack from the horn and set it on the ground. He tied the horse's reins to the animal in front of it. Then he walked to his own horse, mounted, and rode away, as silent as could be, with nary a good-bye.

Maggie was thunderstruck. If she could have done anything to stop him, she would have. But she had already given him her mother's jeweled necklace in payment and there was certainly no point in chasing after him on foot. So she just stood, watching the packtrain disappear down the trail.

Maggie stood for some time, collecting her wits. She looked up the trail that hugged the mountainside. Then she looked at the sun, dipping low in the sky. It would be night before long. A shadow of fear began to creep through her.

Then she brightened. After all, hadn't she come nearly two hundred miles in the last two weeks? Hadn't she ridden the wearying trails and spent the

5

night in mosquito-infested campsites along the way? She guessed, after all, that she could walk the last mile by herself. She swung her bag onto her hip and started up the trail up along the mountainside, through a thick hemlock woods. The trees rose like dark columns all around her. The heat of the day had lifted now, replaced by a cooling quietness.

Suddenly the silence was broken by the cawing of a pair of crows who flew over the treetops, warning the rest of the forest that Maggie was coming. Maggie tilted her head back and smiled. It was then that she realized she had left her bonnet tied to the saddle horn of the horse. But that didn't matter now; Franny would help her make a new one.

She walked for some time. Finally, up ahead, through the trees, she saw a clearing of land on the shoulder of the mountain. In the center of the clearing sat a modest log cabin. It was just as Franny had described in her letters, with walls of solid hewn logs, a hemlock bark roof, and a real stone chimney. The front door was standing open, as if in welcome.

Maggie suddenly felt a terrible weight lifted from her. She was home now! She was really home! She dropped her bag and dashed out into the clearing, knowing that in a moment she would be swept up into the warm and welcoming arms of her aunt Franny.

She burst inside the cabin—and stopped cold.

What she saw made her heart turn to ice.

The cabin was empty.

There were a few broken pieces of crockery scattered about on the dirt floor. A torn piece of blanket hung from the rafters overhead. Branches and leaves had been blown in through the open door and were piled deep in the corners of the room. Maggie could tell that no one had lived there for a long time.

Maggie walked outside. There weren't more than a few armloads of firewood in the woodpile. Out back she could see where a space had been cleared for a garden. But nothing stood there now except a few of last year's dried cornstalks. They rustled in the wind and made a lonely sound.

Knowing it was a foolish thing to do, Maggie cupped her hands around her mouth and shouted off into the forest, "Franny? Franny? Uncle Thomas?" But her voice just died away in the stillness.

Maggie looked down. An old wooden bucket lay on its side in the weeds. She turned it over, sat down on it, and put her chin in her palm.

A bright thought flashed into her mind. She leaped up, stood in the doorway, and called out again. Maybe the neighbors would hear her cries and come up to fetch her. Maybe they would know where Franny was. Then Maggie remembered from Franny's letters that the nearest neighbors were the family at the mill down along Sinking Creek, and that was over a mile away.

A darker thought crept into her mind: Maybe her cries would attract animals, mountain lions or black bears, or maybe even a traveling hunting party of Iroquois Indians. For the first time since she had left Philadelphia, Maggie felt afraid.

It was then that she had the eerie feeling that she was being watched. She felt as though someone was behind her. She spun around and there, standing just a few paces away, was the wildest-looking man Maggie had ever seen.

He stood among the waving corn, stock-still. At first Maggie thought he was an Indian. Then she noticed that he had a long gray beard that trailed down the front of his hunting shirt. His hair was the same color, shoulder length and unruly. He was very old. He was dressed entirely in smoke-stained buckskins. A red-handled tomahawk and a sheath knife with a deer-antler handle were thrust into the woven sash he wore at his waist. Hanging at his right side were his hunting pouch and powder horn. Clasped in his hands was a Pennsylvania long rifle, slanting up and away into the darkness. On his head was a cap made from black bear fur, with a single red-tailed hawk feather that tossed in the breeze as he stood watching her.

But it was his eyes that scared Maggie the most. Peering out from under bushy eyebrows, they were sharp and angry. And cold as gray river ice.

THE OLD MAN STOOD out in the clearing for a long time, staring at Maggie. She was too frightened to move. When he finally spoke, his voice came out loud and gruff, like the growl of an old bear.

"Are you a crazy girl?" he asked.

Maggie would have spoke, but she couldn't get any voice up out of her throat, so she just shook her head.

"Well, tell me this," he said, "if you're not a crazy girl, what're you doin' hollerin' off inta the woods like a crazy girl for?"

Maggie managed to get some voice out of her throat this time, but it came out quavery and meek.

"Well," she started, "I was all by myself here and I was hoping someone would hear me if I shouted just as loud as I could—"

"I heared you," the old man said, cutting her off, "and so did all the deer on the mountainside." He set the butt of his rifle down on the ground and pointed with his chin to the high ground.

"Jest covered with deer trails up there. Them deer come down through this clearing every evenin' at about this time. Come to drink at that spring over there. So, knowin' that, I been waitin' by that spring, waitin' for a good long time, bein' jest as quiet as I kin be, hopin' the forest would send me a deer tonight. Then some crazy girl comes along and starts shoutin' off inta the woods."

Maggie swallowed hard. "Well, I'm sorry. I didn't realize—"

"Where you from anyways, to be so uneducated?"

"From Philadelphia."

"Well, go back there. We don't need any crazy girls hollerin' off inta the woods around here."

Maggie took a deep breath. "But you don't understand. You see, my name is—"

"I don't care what your name is," the old man hissed. "You don't go shoutin' off inta the woods like that. Ruins the huntin'."

"I wish Franny were here," Maggie said to herself.

10

"What would you know about Franny Callahan?" the old man asked.

"That's what I've been trying to tell you! I'm Franny's niece, Maggie. I came here to live with her. Came all this way and now it looks like she's not here. Do you know where she is?"

The old man shook his head and chuckled. "So. You're Maggie, eh? She spoke about you. Why didn't you say so in the first place?"

"Well, I tried to, but every time I—"

The old man raised his hand. "Now, that's all right, you don't have ta explain—I sp'ose you're kinda turned inside out about all this. Well, I'll give it to you as di-rect as I ken. Your aunt Franny and uncle Thomas pulled up stakes and headed out to the Ohio Valley about four months ago, jest after the spring thaw."

Maggie shook her head.

"She wouldn't do that without writing me. She would want me to know where she was."

He nodded. "She probably did. But it could take six months or more fer that letter to git to ya. And even if she did write ya, how would she know where she was goin'? That's all wild country out there, girl. You could wander over that territory your whole life and never find 'em. When folks go west like that, they're gen'rally gone for good, never ta be seen again."

"Well, what am I going to do?"

"Do? Well, girl, there's only one thing to do. We're jest gonna have ta set out tomorrow and I'm gonna have ta traipse you back downstream to the Susquehanna, get you on a boat back to Philadelphy, where you belong. Thomas and Franny were like brother and sister to me. I'll do what I ken to see you back safely."

"But I can't go back," Maggie protested. "I haven't got anything to go back to."

"No fambly?"

Maggie shook her head. "Mama died of the fever three weeks ago and Papa's been away at sea for two years," she said, her voice quavering. "And I have no brothers or sisters. Why, Franny's practically my only living relative."

"Well, only livin' relative or not, you got ta go back. No place fer a civilized girl like you out here. So back you go—I don't want to hear any more about it." The old man scratched his chin whiskers. "I jest got one question."

"What's that?"

"How in Lucifer's name did you get out here in the first place?"

Maggie sighed. "That's a long story."

The old man pushed his cap back on his head. "Well, I got all night. Nothin' to do now that the deer been run off."

The hunter slapped his leg. "But listen now, we can make jaw music about this later. You hungry?"

Maggie nodded. She was suddenly very hungry. Mr. Johnson's cooking hadn't been anything to rave about. The cornmeal mush he had made at dawn still lay like a dollop of lead in her stomach.

The hunter glanced around the clearing. "Well, we'll go inside and pull together a meal. You get that bucket yer settin' on and fetch us up some water from that spring over there. I'll go inside and strike up a fire."

When Maggie returned to the cabin with the heavy bucket of water, she could see the old man kneeling down by the hearth, laying out his fire-making gear: a chunk of flint, a bar of striking steel, a square of charred cotton cloth, and a handful of tinder made from the fluffed-up inner bark of the willow tree. He had already built a small pyramid of hemlock twigs in the fireplace, ready to receive the fire when he had it going.

Maggie watched intently as he placed a thumbnail-sized square of charred cloth on the top of the flint, holding it down with the thumb of his left hand. He struck the edge of the rock a glancing blow with the steel bar. A shower of sparks flew up into the darkness. One landed on the charred cloth and began to glow orange. The old man picked up the tinder bundle in one hand and carefully inserted the glowing

13

cloth into its center. Then he held the tinder aloft and blew. Smoke began curling up, and a moment later the bundle burst into flames. Quickly, he tucked the flaming bark in among the hemlock twigs. The fire crackled to life. He added larger twigs, then branches. Then he turned to Maggie and said one word, "Wood."

She ducked outside and brought in all the wood she could salvage from the woodpile. She went back out and fetched her traveling bag, which lay at the edge of the clearing where she had dropped it. When she came back inside, she was glad for the firelight. The cabin seemed almost cheerful now.

In no time the old man had prepared a simple meal of hot sassafras tea and jerked deer meat. He found a wooden bowl on the floor, filled it with tea, and passed it to Maggie. She took the bowl in both hands and drank. It tasted hot and strong. She sat back against the cabin wall, drank the rest of the tea, and chewed hard on a strip of jerky he handed her.

"A body travels these mountains by hisself for so long, he gets hungry for talk," the old man was saying. "You mind conversin' for a while?"

Maggie smiled. "No, I don't mind." She was a little hungry for talk herself. Herbert Johnson hadn't been much of a conversationalist.

"So tell me how you come to this valley," he asked.

"Came by horseback," Maggie said. "First across the level road from Philadelphia to Lancaster, then

14

on to Paxtang on the banks of the Susquehanna River. We crossed at Clark's Ferry, then headed up the west bank to the mouth of the Juniata River. We ferried across and kept to the north bank of the Juniata right up into the mountains. We rode up over the mountain ridges, all seven of them, and came down into the Great Valley just about sundown tonight."

"You keep sayin' 'we.' Who'd you come with?"

"A man by the name of Herbert Johnson, mountain tinker."

The old man nodded. "I've heard the name. But how'd you get hooked up with him? That is, if you don't mind me askin'."

"No, I don't mind," Maggie said in a weary voice. "I guess it can't do any harm to tell you.

"Mama died and no one knew exactly where Papa was, so some folks from the church said they'd take me in as a hired girl and I could work for my keep. Do kitchen and garden work. Which would have been all right. And I was ready to go, too. But as I was packing up, I ran across the letters Franny had sent since she moved out here.

"Franny and I were always real close. When Mama took sick years ago, Franny came to live with us in Philadelphia. Meanwhile Uncle Thomas came here to lay out a homestead. A few years later Franny joined him.

"That's when the letters started to come. Maybe

two or three times a year, Franny would pay Herbert Johnson to carry me a letter when he came back to Philadelphia for supplies.

"And, oh, I used to live for those letters. From the first time that I heard about this valley, I wanted to come out here and live with Franny.

"Anyway, I found these letters while I was packing up and I realized that I didn't want to move into some stranger's house and be a hired-out girl. I wanted to come here and live with Franny. She was the one I felt closest to anyway. With Mama so sick all the time and Papa away so much, it was almost as if Franny was both mother and father to me.

"I remembered that one time Mr. Johnson told me that if I ever wanted to pay him to carry a letter back to Franny, I could always leave word at the stable where he kept his horses. So I went down there and found him. Just by luck he was just about to leave on another trip west. So I talked him into bringing me out here. He said I'd have to pay him real well because of the added risk of transporting a runaway. So I did. I gave him Mama's sapphire necklace—real jewels, you know."

Maggie bit her lower lip.

"I sure hated to give up that necklace. She wore it the day she and Papa were married. She said she was saving it for me. She had to sell off the rest of her jewelry for medicine, but she always kept that one—

the blue sapphire, saying I'd wear it on my own wedding day."

Maggie stared into the fire, feeling the loss.

"So, you see, I really can't go back to Philadelphia. I guess they figure me like lost property. I think they'd whip me good if they could get me back now."

The old man warmed his moccasins by the fire.

"That was very brave, girl, takin' things inta yer own hands like that," he said, "but takin' a whippin' would be better'n starvin' or freezin' ta death up on this mountainside. So back you go, girl, and that's all there is to it."

Maggie decided to let the matter rest for now.

"I never even asked your name," she said.

"I'm just an old man," he said. "I don't need a name anymore. But those who talk to me call me by my given name."

"What's that?"

"Jake Logan. That's the name my mother give me. But most folks around here don't care to talk to me anyway."

"Why's that?"

The old man laughed to himself. "You could say I'm a mite unpopular around here. They don't take to wild men or wild critters, us that's been trampin' this valley long before they laid eyes on it. See, they plan to civilize this country, and that kinda thinkin' doesn't leave much room for people like me.

17

" 'Course your aunt and uncle were never that way. No, they were folks that knew how to live and let be. They were friends—I'd say only friends I had in this valley." Jake settled back against the cabin wall. "Had many a fine meal inside these walls," he said. "Many a fine meal. Your aunt was a good woman, you know. Likely, she still is. She sure had a way with people. Why, even the most cantankerous souls would warm up to her. That was partly 'cause of the way she was. And partly because of the bread, a' course."

"What do you mean?"

"Well, Franny was known far and wide for that bread of hers. She would bake up that Callahan bread and people would just flock to it. Why, people'd move heaven and earth for that bread. Got to be so them loaves was good as money in these parts. Franny would bake 'em up and trade 'em for things she and Thomas needed. Many's the time I brought 'em squirrels and rabbits ta exchange fer that bread.

"No, we never had a bread like Franny's, not before or since. It rised up light and airy and thick-crusted at the same time. Made a man's mouth glad ta chomp inta it!"

The old man's lips began to work reminiscently.

"She was like a sister," the man said quietly, "the way she listened to folks' troubles and pains and baked the bread for 'em. Some people called her the Bread Sister, because that's just what she was. She

18

was like a sister ta everybody."

The old man had a faraway look in his eyes. When he turned his gaze to Maggie, he could see she had been sitting wide-eyed, taking in every word.

Jake suddenly felt embarrassed, as though he had talked too long and too openly with this young girl. He slapped his buckskinned thigh and stood up.

"Well, now," he said, "we best get some sleep. We have to make tracks tomorrow. I'll set out first thing in the mornin' and get us some meat for the trip—be back by noon at the latest. You stick close to the cabin 'til I get back. You can sleep in here by the fire, I'll bed down outside under the stars. That smoke will keep most of the bugs off you."

He gathered up his rifle and hunting pouch and stepped silently out into the darkness, leaving the door open behind him.

Maggie settled back against the cabin wall. It had been a long day and she was very tired. Through the open doorway, somewhere up along the mountainside, she heard the lonely call of a night bird, but she had no way of knowing what kind it was.

MAGGIE LAY BACK ON the dirt floor by the hearth and fell asleep, fell into the deep sleep that weary people know, the sleep that gives way to dreams.

She dreamed that she was back in her parents' house in Philadelphia. Her father was away at sea, as he often was. Her mother, who was very ill, was asleep in her bed upstairs.

Maggie was sitting with her aunt Franny before the hearth in the kitchen. In the dream, Maggie could see her aunt—a tall, sturdy woman with a sure, strong way about her. Her red, red hair was twisted up into the bun she wore at the back of her head. The firelight flickered across her face, showing the lines that living had put there.

Maggie knew this dream. It was one she often had. It was the remembrance of something that had happened years before, something that had changed the girl's life forever.

Franny dried her hands off on her apron and took a deep breath before she spoke.

"Maggie," she said in her rough Irish brogue, "there's somethin' I've been meanin' to tell ye. I'm goin' away very soon . . . and I don't know that I'll ever be back."

Maggie smiled, as if she were hearing a joke. "What do you mean? You've always lived here. And you always will. You've lived here as long as I can remember."

"No, dear, it only seems that way. The time's really been very short. Now it's time for me to go."

Maggie began to realize that her aunt wasn't joking.

"You remember your uncle Thomas," Franny went on. "You'll remember how he came over from Ireland on the boat with me and you'll remember that he went west two years ago to build a homestead on the frontier? You'll remember all that, won't you, Maggie?"

The girl nodded slowly.

"Well, I got a letter from him this mornin' and he

wants me to come over and join him when the spring thaw comes. He's got us a cabin on forty acres of land out there. And Maggie, I have to go. 'Tis two years now since I saw my husband and I want a farm of me own. I know that's hard for a young girl to understand. But maybe in time ye will. What's that look on your face now, dear?"

"I was just thinking," Maggie answered, "I was just thinking how different this house will be without you here. With Papa gone so much and Mama weaker than ever and just me here alone." Maggie began to cry. "I don't want to be here alone. Don't leave me, I want to go with you." She buried her head in the older woman's lap. Franny gently stroked the girl's hair.

"I know, dear, I know. If you were my own, I'd take ye with me in a minute. Don't think I haven't thought about it. But when I'm gone, your mother will need you more than ever. And, sure the frontier is no place for a young girl like yerself. Ye'll be wantin' to be near parties and dances before long now. There's none of that out there, just hard work, Maggie. And, good God, if somethin' ever happened to ye, yer mother would never forgive me."

"I don't care about all that," Maggie said. "I just want to go with you."

"Now, don't go on like that," Franny said. She

took Maggie by the shoulders and held her firm, looking into her eyes.

" 'Tis not the end for me and you, sure. I'll write every so often. And I want ye to know where'er ye go, I'll always be with ye child, I'll always be with ye in spirit. Won't ye remember that, Maggie?"

The girl nodded, tears rolling down her cheeks.

"Now," Franny said briskly, "I've got somethin' here for ye, sort of a goin'-away present, from me to you."

Franny reached down into the bosom of her dress and drew out an old leather pouch that hung around her neck by a leather thong. The pouch was about the size of Maggie's fist. Franny held the pouch up in the firelight.

"Inside this pouch," Franny said, "is the most precious thing I can give ye. 'Tis somethin' that's been in the family many years. 'Tis the Great Callahan Spook Yeast."

Maggie wrinkled her brow. "I never heard of it before."

"Rightly so, dear. You never heard because 'tis our family secret."

"Spook yeast," Maggie repeated the phrase. "Why's it called that?"

Franny laughed, "That's what me mother, God rest her, always used to call it. Because it's got a life of its own, I suppose, like a spook."

"What's it good for?" the girl asked.

"Good for? To bake bread, o' course. I never showed ye this before, but the spook yeast is the secret to bakin' the Callahan bread that you know so well. This bakin' secret has been passed down by the women in our family since God knows when. And now 'tis time for you to learn, Maggie. Ye come by it honest. Yer a Callahan yerself."

Maggie's eyes glowed with wonder.

" 'Tis the yeasties inside this pouch that do the trick," Franny was saying. She dipped her fingers into the pouch and pinched off a roll of what looked like bread dough. She held it in her palm by the firelight.

"A loaf of bread without spook yeast is just as hard and flat as a brick. 'Tis a livin' thing, Maggie. If ye add a cup of this spook yeast to yer bread dough, the yeast creatures start workin' in the dough and the bread comes to life too."

"Smells sour," Maggie said.

"Aye, 'tis the smell of the yeasties workin'," said Franny. "The original Callahan spook yeast was nothin' but flour and water allowed to sour in the heat. That starts the yeasties to growin'. But this mixture has gained somethin' more by bein' passed down all those years. 'Tis the aging that's made the spook yeast what it is. Some say ye can trace this yeast back for seven generations in the Callahan family. And 'tis still goin', still alive."

"But why do you wear it around your neck like that?" Maggie asked.

"Because, dear, the yeasties are livin' things; ye got to keep 'em warm. Too much heat kills them; too much cold puts them to sleep. The warmth of your body is just right. So I wear it around me neck, as all the Callahan women have, to keep it safe and warm as it should be.

" 'Tis the closest thing the Callahans have to an inheritance, Maggie. And now 'tis time it came to you."

Franny reached into the pocket that hung at her apron and pulled out another leather pouch, which looked exactly like hers except that it was new.

As Maggie watched, Franny pinched out half of her own spook yeast and combined it with a cup of flour and water she had mixed and set by the fire. The tangy sour aroma of the spook yeast began to fill the kitchen. To Maggie it seemed as though she was watching magic at work.

Franny rolled the doughy mixture into a ball and placed it in Maggie's pouch, then pulled the drawstring tight.

"Come sit by me here, Maggie," Franny said. The older woman held the pouch by the leather thong and settled it down over Maggie's head so the pouch lay like a necklace on the girl's chest. "I pass the spook yeast to you, Maggie," Franny said. Maggie

25

reached up and felt the pleasant roundness and full-
ness of the bag in her hand.

"It feels alive," she said.

"Aye," Franny nodded. " 'Tis, dear, 'tis. Keep it
safe around yer neck and the life of the bread will
never leave ye. I'll teach ye the bread-bakin' secrets
before I leave, dear. Take care of it and ye'll get many
a loaf of bread out of that pouch. I have a feelin' that
the bread bakin' will give ye a place in the world,
Maggie. 'Tis somethin' of strength I can leave ye. So
follow your nose, Maggie—"

"I know," the girl said. "I know what you always
say, 'Follow your nose—and don't be afraid of
nothin'.' "

"Rightly so, Maggie," Franny said. Then she
stopped for a moment and thought. " 'Tis the rule
I've lived by all me days. But that doesn't mean the
same will work for you. 'Tis up to ye to make yer own
rules, then stay to them. That's not always as easy as
it sounds.

"You see, Maggie, you and I are different. The
adventurous life is not for you. Yer a quiet soul,
Maggie, but ye got the strength of the Callahans
within ye.

"I've got the notion that someday ye'll be put to
the test, like God tests us all. I think the most important thing for you to learn is not to *follow* your nose,
as I have, but to look *past* your nose, to really *see*

what yer lookin' at. Does that make any sense to ye?"

Maggie nodded.

" 'Twill make more sense as time goes by," Franny said.

Then the dream faded away.

When Maggie opened her eyes, she found herself lying on the dirt floor in the cabin up on the mountainside.

In the eerie moments between sleeping and waking, Maggie wasn't sure whether she had just been with Franny or not. Then her head cleared and she realized that it had all been a dream and that Franny was out west somewhere, hundreds of miles away.

Maggie looked outside. It was very dark. Dark as midnight. Seeking some light to comfort herself, the girl picked up a dead hemlock branch, with the dried needles still clinging to it, and tossed it onto the glowing embers of the fire. The branch burst into flames. The firelight leaped and danced on the cabin walls.

Maggie sat back against the wall and looked over the cabin. It was as though she were seeing it for the first time. Even in its run-down state, she could tell that Franny had once lived there.

The entire western wall was dominated by a huge stone fireplace Uncle Thomas must have built to Franny's careful specifications. The main chamber of the fireplace allowed plenty of room for hanging stewpots or setting up a roasting spit that could be used to turn and brown a duck over the coals.

Then Maggie spotted Franny's bake oven—a square chamber set into the rock wall. Maggie knew how carefully it had been constructed. It was similar to the one they'd used in Philadelphia. She knew the inside was bell-shaped and that the inner walls were plastered with clay, baked to rocklike hardness. She knew the bricks that formed the floor and walls of the oven were carefully made from pressed clay gathered from the creekbank. She knew all this without having to look inside.

Maggie rose and walked across the room, placing her hand on the rough stone around the oven. And there, standing propped up in the shadowy corner just as the older woman had left it, she saw Franny's peel. Maggie knew that this long-handled, paddlelike tool was what Franny had used to lift her bread loaves in and out of the baking oven. She reached for it. It felt good and smooth to the touch. Uncle Thomas must have carved it from hard maple.

Maggie had an eerie feeling holding Franny's peel. It was almost as though she felt the physical presence of her aunt nearby. Then the dream flashed into her mind. And she remembered Franny's words.

"Look past my nose," Maggie said to herself. "Now what's that supposed to mean?"

Her eyes fell on her traveling sack, which lay

against the cabin wall. She thought about how carefully she had packed it the night she had left Philadelphia. She had included things she thought she would need—an extra change of clothes and a few cooking provisions. But she had never gotten to use any of them. She sighed at the thought of carrying that heavy bag all the way back to Philadelphia with her.

She realized that the heaviest thing of all was the ten-pound bag of wheat flour she had brought, figuring to make bread on the trail. She thought about the other provisions that would go to waste—the bag of salt, the crock of honey. She thought about her bread knife, sharpened and stowed away in its canvas sheath—all things that wouldn't be used.

Suddenly Maggie really did see what she was looking at. She looked down at the peel in her hands, then back at the traveling bag.

"No," she thought, "it won't go to waste. I've got everything here I need to bake bread. I'll carry that flour back as bread loaves."

From there on out, Maggie moved without thinking. Her hands and mind did all the things that needed to be done, as though she were guided by some strong inner force.

She threw another branch on the fire and set to work. She knew that she must first mix her spook yeast starter. Maggie dipped into her pouch and pinched out a generous ball of spook yeast, added a few drops of honey, and set it to ferment by the fire. She mixed her bread dough right in the flour bag by adding some water from the bucket and kneading the mixture with her hands.

She took her clean apron out of the bag and spread it across an old wooden box. She dusted the surface of the apron with flour, then rolled the huge ball of bread dough out onto it. The yeasty smells of the starter had begun to fill the cabin. Maggie thought of nothing but the bread. She added the spook yeast to the dough, knowing the life of the yeasties would now sink into the dough. She rolled it into a big ball, covered it with her apron, and set it near the hearth to rise. It would be ready by dawn.

Maggie suddenly felt tired. She lay down on the floor by the hearth and fell instantly asleep, knowing she would be rising early to stoke the baking fire.

At dawn Maggie began her baking fire by scraping a few glowing coals onto a piece of wood and carefully transferring the embers to the bake oven. She used all the wood lying around the cabin to build on that fire until it was a roaring blaze. When she went outside for more wood, she saw no sign of the old man. She knew he must have gone hunting already.

When Maggie piled on the split hardwood, the flames shot up the flue with a roaring sound, like wind howling on a winter night. It was good, Maggie thought, knowing she needed to get the bricks inside the oven red-hot before the bread could be baked.

While the fire roared, Maggie checked her dough. It had risen overnight, as the spook yeast worked within it. She kneaded the bread down, using the familiar motions Franny had taught her so long ago. She felt the dough spring back under her hands, taking on a life of its own. She felt Franny's spirit working with her on the dough. And she remembered what her aunt had said: "I'll always be with ye in spirit, Maggie."

Maggie rolled the dough up into three perfectly round loaves, then covered them and set them by the fire to rise a second time.

She was sweating freely now. The fire in the bake oven made the room quite hot, even though Maggie had the door propped open.

The oven was ready. Maggie used a branch to rake the burning wood from the oven and sweep it into the fireplace. Then, with a water-soaked rag wrapped around the end of a stick, she swabbed the inside of the oven clean of dirt and ashes.

Maggie peered into the fierce heat of the oven. The bricks radiated an incredible amount of heat. She used the last of the flour to dust the paddle of the peel and the floor of the oven so the dough wouldn't stick to those surfaces. The last thing she did before placing the loaves in the oven was to use her sharp knife to cut a cross into the top of each loaf—"to put the blessin' of God on the bread," as Franny used to say.

She lifted the loaves onto the peel and, ever so gently, slid them into the scorching heat of the oven. She sprinkled water on the wooden oven door to keep it from burning and lifted it into place, closing the oven up. She knew the loaves would bake quickly now, browning and doubling in size.

Maggie wiped the sweat from her face with the corner of her apron and walked out into the cool air. It was already midmorning. She felt the sun coming up into the clearing, casting off the dark shadows made by the towering hemlocks. She sat on the doorstep to rest.

A thought floated into Maggie's mind. Franny had always told her that if something was troubling her and she couldn't find an answer on her own, she should take her troubles to the bread. That was exactly what Maggie had done. She had taken her troubles to the bread. And in working the dough, an answer had come to her. It was so simple, she was surprised she hadn't thought of it before.

SHORTLY BEFORE NOON, Jake came back to the cabin with two squirrels and a string of fish slung over his back. As he was coming into the clearing, his nose began to twitch.

"That's the Callahan bread," he said to himself. He quickened his pace. The old man came through the cabin door just in time to see Maggie pull the last of the rounded golden loaves from the bake oven. Jake's mouth dropped open.

"Girl," he said at last, "I didn't know you had the bread-bakin' gift! Whyn't you tell me?"

"Well," Maggie said, "I didn't think it was important."

"Not important! Girl, I haven't had a decent taste of bread since Franny left and you think it's not important!"

The old man knelt down and examined the bread loaves.

As Jake watched, Maggie cut a steaming slice and handed it to him. He took the bread and held it under his nose with his eyes closed, bathing his weathered face in the fragrant smell. He took a bite, eyes closed, chewing like a man who had died and gone to heaven.

"It's the Callahan bread," Jake said, "sure as any Franny ever baked."

Jake silently devoured slice after slice until he had eaten almost half a loaf.

"Don't eat so much," Maggie warned him. "Hot bread's not so good for your stomach."

Jake patted his belly. "Right you are, girl, right you are. Jest tastes so good, a man fergits himself."

Maggie had a piece of bread. It did taste good hot, she had to admit.

"Jake," she said, "I've been thinking. What was it people used to call my aunt?"

The old man brushed the crumbs off his beard.

"Oh, you mean 'the Bread Sister.' "

"The Bread Sister," Maggie said the words to herself, to get the feel of them.

"And you said her bread was as good as money in

this valley, and that she would trade for things she needed?"

"That she would, girl. That she would. Like I said, people'd move heaven and earth for that bread."

"Well then, why don't I do that?"

The old man stopped chewing. "Do what?"

"What you said. Why don't I stay on here and bake the bread and trade for the things I need to live? I could take Franny's place as the Bread Sister."

"I was right," Jake said. "You *are* a crazy girl. Now, as much as I'd love ta have you here bakin' this bread regular, I still know in my bones that that would be a bad idee."

"But why?"

"Well, lotsa reasons," Jake said. "Oh, now your aunt could make it that way, it's true. But she had quite a few things in her favor, you know."

"Like what?"

"Well, first off, she didn't have to do it alone. She had a man, which you don't, and a good one at that. Second, Franny was a growed woman, which you ain't."

"I know about hard work," Maggie put in.

The old man shook his head, "Even allowin' that, yer still jest a girl and a lightweight at that. Franny knew how to do things you can't even imagine. She could skin a squirrel, chop a load of firewood, even fire a flintlock if need be. You know how to do all them things?"

Maggie shook her head.

"No, I didn't think so. And all that wouldn't be so bad, girl. Except that you have no way of knowin' what it gets like up in these mountains come winter. It ain't like settin' up housekeepin' in Philadelphia. Why, I've lived in these mountains for years now and I'm still thankful when every spring rolls around and I'm here to see it. Now you think you're gonna master all them skills I been learnin' all my borned days? You think you're gonna learn all that before the first snow flies?

"No, Maggie, it would be a cruelty for me to pretend you could. Franny would skin me alive if she ever found out I let you freeze er starve ta death up on this mountainside. So back you go, bread bakin' er not!"

Just then a shadow fell across the doorway, blocking out the morning light. The old man and the girl turned and saw someone standing in the doorway.

He was huge. Not just tall, but broad and solid like an oak barrel. Even though he was dressed simply in a farmer's shirt, vest, and knee breeches, Maggie noticed that he had his hair carefully arranged into a fashionable queue plaited down the back of his neck. His face was flushed red and his eyes, peering through spectacles perched on his nose, were wide and angry.

In his hand was a flintlock dueling pistol, pointed directly at Jake's chest.

"Don't move, Mr. Logan." His voice sounded overly loud in the tiny cabin. He stepped over the doorsill and into the room. As he did, his spectacles slid down his nose and he had to poke them back up again. The big man shifted his eyes to Maggie. He motioned to her with his free hand.

"Well, child, don't just stand there like a duck in a thunderstorm. Move over here by me. I'll protect you."

Maggie didn't know what to do.

"Has he harmed you?" the man asked.

Maggie shook her head.

"Well, it's fortunate for you that I happened by. This man could have done you great harm. He is the only criminal who inhabits this valley and the only human danger we face. Except, of course, for the red savages."

It was then that the big man caught sight of the string of fish and squirrels hanging from the rafters, where Jake had left them.

"Ah," he said, "poaching again?" He gave a high, hysterical laugh that filled the cabin. "I've caught you red-handed, you rapscallion, and now you will receive the punishment you so richly deserve.

"I have among my papers at the house a formal complaint drawn up by the leading citizens of this valley. You seem to have a poor understanding of property rights. We are landholders in this valley now. That means that we own not just the land but everything upon it—the plants, the animals, even the water that flows in the ground."

He gestured with the pistol.

"The days are over, Mr. Logan, when you can wander the valley at will, shooting animals and picking apples and frightening people with your rude and uncivilized ways.

"So, by the power vested in me as deputy constable, I will now escort you to General Potter's house, where you will receive thirty lashes at the public whipping post."

Maggie cut her eyes back to Jake to see how he was taking all this.

"Better watch that pistol," Jake said evenly. "It could go off and hurt someone."

The big man glanced down at the pistol, then quickly back at Jake. It was then that his nostrils caught the scent of the bread.

"Is that bread I smell?" he asked.

"Yes, it is," Maggie spoke up. "I baked it. You see, my name is—"

"Whatever your name is, young lady, you are safe with me. I can't help but wonder about the bread though." His eyes fell on the loaves.

"These rounded, golden loaves, they remind me of Franny's bread." His eyes glazed over. He seemed to have forgotten the pistol in his hand. "Haven't had any bread here for—how long is it, now?"

Maggie stooped and sliced him a steaming chunk and carried it to him. The man popped it into his cavernous mouth and began chewing with his eyes closed.

It was at that moment that Jake made his move. He silently slid across the room, snatched up his rifle, and was gone.

Maggie saw it all.

"Ah, yes," the man was saying, "food of the gods. I have always said to my good wife Maura, there is nothing like fresh-baked bread to make a house a ho—" He opened his eyes and glanced around. "Now where is that rapscallion?"

He grew even redder in the face and turned and dashed out the doorway. He glanced around the borders of the clearing.

"Logan!" he bellowed. "I know you're out there. I know you can hear me." He shook his fist at the trees. "I swear to you that this is not the end. I swear, by the trust the citizens of this community have placed in me, I will bring you to the whipping post. There is justice in this valley!"

His oration finished, the man heaved a great sigh

and stepped back into the cabin. He sat down on the doorstep and began wiping his forehead with an enormous handkerchief.

"He's eluded me again," the man said. Then he glanced up at Maggie and stood up rather formally.

"I know this all must be quite confusing to you," he said. "Allow me to introduce myself. I am Joseph McGrew. I own the mill down on Sinking Creek. I was Franny's nearest neighbor.

"When I saw the chimney smoke this morning, I thought Franny might be back. So I came up here to investigate. A deputy constable must pay attention to these things, you know. You aren't hurt in any way then?"

Maggie shook her head.

"Good. Now perhaps you will answer some questions for me. Who are you and what brings you to this green and verdant valley?"

Maggie took a deep breath. "My name is Maggie Callahan and I came here from Philadelphia to live with my aunt Franny—"

"Ah, yes, Philadelphia. I remember it well. My wife and I used to be on the great stage in Philadelphia." He sang a snatch of an aria, very loudly and very terribly. "Unfortunately, we encountered a few hostile audiences. Maura and I were obliged to leave town on short notice."

He swept his arms in an impressive gesture.

"Then we turned our faces to the challenge of the frontier. We've built a home here in the savage wilderness. And this will be a great community someday. With banks and churches and schools. And places of culture, too. Where I can personally perform the works of the great playwrights for the delighted audiences of the future. Now, of course, I'm heavily involved in the mill business—but that's only a phase in the great master plan. After all, don't you think there's as much good to be done in business and politics as in the arts?"

Maggie nodded.

Then McGrew clapped a hand to his forehead.

"But what am I thinking of? Here I am, rambling on, and you must be fatigued. Come down to the house with me now. Any visitor is a treat to us. Especially a Callahan who brings such delicious breadstuffs to our table." McGrew suddenly stopped himself. "Forgive me. You don't mind bringing these to our table do you?"

Maggie shook her head. She was very confused by all of this. She remembered Franny had mentioned McGrew in her letters and said that he was a good man. So she gathered up the extra loaves in her apron and picked up her nearly empty traveling bag. McGrew picked up the string of game.

"By the way," McGrew said, "you do know about your aunt and uncle moving on, don't you?"

Maggie nodded. "Jake Logan told me."

"Just as well," McGrew said, "I hate breaking bad news."

They walked down the path toward Sinking Creek. On the way, McGrew asked about Maggie's circumstances in coming to the valley. He talked about his theatrical career. As they strolled along, he sang in a loud voice. Birds and squirrels scattered before him as he walked. Maggie wondered what Jake would say about McGrew's way of traveling in the woods. But then, she thought, there were probably a lot of things the two men disagreed about.

WHEN MAGGIE SAW SINKING CREEK for the first time, she was surprised at how small it was. In some places the creek was so narrow that a nimble person could easily leap across it. But it was clear and ran with a musical tone.

Maggie and McGrew came into a clearing, and Maggie could see that the stream had been dammed into a pond. The mill was reflected in the still water of the pond. It was a huge impressive structure with an enormous wooden waterwheel.

As they walked, McGrew explained that the runoff from the pond was channeled down a long wooden chute where a steady stream fell onto the water-wheel, turning it smoothly. The motion of the wheel turned the grindstones inside, which ground rye and corn into rye flour and cornmeal. McGrew said in the winter the same power was used to propel the up-and-down motion of a saw-toothed blade in the sawmill out back.

As they drew closer, Maggie could see the main house, set up away from the pond a bit. It was a tranquil scene.

"Let me show you my pride and joy," McGrew said hospitably. He took Maggie into the mill and she marveled at the maze of wooden cogwheels that turned the heavy grindstones. The mill was not oper-ating at the moment. McGrew excused himself to climb up and check the works.

Maggie was so impressed by the massive wooden machinery that she didn't notice the little girl who had walked up beside her. Maggie turned and, sud-denly, there was the girl, appeared seemingly out of nowhere. She looked about twelve years old. She had jet-black hair and very delicate hands and feet.

"Hello," Maggie said. "What's your name?"

The girl smiled. With great care, she slowly drew the letter *A* in the air with her finger. Then she drew another letter. An *N*. Another *N*. An *I*. And an *E*.

"Annie," Maggie said, "your name is Annie. I'm Maggie."

Annie gave her a dazzling smile, then reached out and firmly shook her hand.

McGrew climbed down from the loft.

"Ah," he said, "I see you've met my daughter."

"She's very clever with her hands," Maggie said. "She spelled her name out in the air for me. I'd like to hear her voice."

"That's her way of talking," McGrew said sadly.

"What do you mean?"

"Our girl Annie can't speak or hear. Several years ago, she was in a terrible accident. Miraculously, the Lord spared her life. But, in His wisdom, He took from her the powers of speech and hearing.

"However, she is a bright girl. And she has devised her own ways of communicating. If you speak slowly, she can read your lips. And she has invented a sort of language of her own, with gestures and hand signs. I daresay, once you get onto her way of signing, you can speak with her about most anything."

Annie touched McGrew on the arm to get his attention. She made a series of graceful motions with her hands and pointed to Maggie.

"She wants to know where you're from and what you're doing here," he explained.

The big man slowly recounted Maggie's story. Annie watched, her eyes riveted to her father's lips. Maggie saw the waves of sadness begin to break

45

across the girl's face as she came to understand Maggie's predicament.

Annie touched her palm to her heart and shook her head.

"She says she feels sad for you," McGrew said. "But listen, no point in dwelling on all this now. What's done is done. You must agree to be our houseguest for the night."

McGrew turned to Annie. "Take Maggie to the house, introduce her to your mother, and ask her if we might have Maggie as our houseguest tonight."

Annie nodded and took Maggie's hand in hers.

As they approached the house, Maggie could see that the McGrews' house was built on a much grander scale than Franny's cabin. The log walls were hewn flat and neatly fitted at the corners. There were two chimneys, one at each end, and a real shingle roof.

As they came closer, a tall woman, dressed entirely in black, wearing a black bonnet that covered most of her face, stepped from the doorway and threw a kettle of filthy water into the weeds.

She heard them approaching and looked up. Her face was in shadow, but Maggie could see beneath the ruffle of the bonnet two dark, sharp eyes peering out at her. The woman simply stood with the kettle in her hands, staring at Maggie as though she had seen a ghost.

"This is Maggie," Annie signed. "She came here from Philadelphia and Papa says to ask can she stay here with us tonight."

Maggie shifted under the woman's gaze.

"Where's your bonnet?" the woman said at last. She spoke to Maggie in a voice that sounded like a whiplash.

"I lost it," Maggie admitted.

"Sensible girl wouldn't be out in the sun without a bonnet," Mrs. McGrew declared.

"Well," Maggie began, trying to sound friendly, "I know that. But you see, my name is—"

"I already know your name," the woman snapped. She pointed to Maggie's clothes.

"Look at your dress. You look like you've been rolling in the dirt. I don't know why my husband insists on taking in every stray traveler in the valley. Well, you won't come in my house that way."

She turned to Annie and made hand motions for washing. Then, for Maggie's benefit, she said, "Take her to the pond. And scrub her good."

Mrs. McGrew turned her gaze back to Maggie. "I don't allow slovenliness in my house." Then she turned and was gone. Her words hung like icicles in the air.

Maggie went to the pond and washed herself with the harsh lye soap Annie brought. Then the younger girl poured a bucket of water over her head, and she washed the dust of the trail from her hair. Annie also brought her a simple sack dress, which Maggie slipped into. She hadn't felt so clean in weeks. It felt good to sit by the pond with her eyes closed, letting the sun dry her as Annie's nimble fingers brushed out her hair and plaited it into two long braids that trailed down her back.

When they returned to the house, the family sat down to supper. It was a simple meal, cold fish and corn, left over from the bigger meal the family ate at noon. But the meal was made grand by the addition of Maggie's bread.

McGrew took his place at the head of the table. Mrs. McGrew had taken off her bonnet now, and Maggie could see from Mrs. McGrew's high cheekbones and graceful aquiline nose that she had once been a beautiful woman. But now, Maggie thought, her face looked pale and tired and very sad.

She glanced around the room and saw that Mrs. McGrew did keep a very clean house. The fireplaces at each end of the house were well stocked with split firewood for cooking; the stone hearths were swept clean. Mr. and Mrs. McGrew's bed, which sat in one corner, was neatly covered with a comfortable quilt. Maggie noticed a ladder going up to the loft overhead where she figured Annie slept.

Then Maggie saw something else. Sitting in the corner by the large bed was a handmade cradle. In the cradle was a sleeping baby.

"Let us bow our heads," McGrew said, and began to say grace over the meal. He had no sooner thanked the Lord for two or three things than the baby started awake and began screaming. Mrs. McGrew wearily left her place at the table and lifted the baby from its cradle. She opened the front of her blouse and nursed the infant. As soon as the child began sucking, its cries quieted.

"Our little boy Lyons is quite ill," McGrew said. "He was a sickly child from the start, and since then it's been just one illness after another. We've come very close to losing him."

McGrew bowed his head and finished his prayer.

"Now," McGrew said with an expansive smile, "let's share in the bounteous wonder of this bread."

Maggie carefully selected a fresh loaf and cut a large slice for each person. Mrs. McGrew put the sleeping baby back in the cradle and came to the table. Maggie watched as the three McGrews sat silently and ate the bread, eating quietly, as though making a sound would somehow interfere with the taste.

McGrew washed the last of his slice down with a mug of cider.

"Well, Maura," he said. "It's the Callahan bread now, isn't it? As fine a loaf as Franny baked."

Mrs. McGrew nodded silently.

After the meal was over, Mrs. McGrew had Maggie do the washing up. While she worked, Maggie was conscious that the older woman was watching her every move.

That evening Maggie and Annie began to climb the ladder to the sleeping loft.

Then Maggie heard Mrs. McGrew's voice saying, "Maggie, come here." Maggie climbed back down the ladder to face Mrs. McGrew.

Mrs. McGrew was sitting in her rocking chair by the hearth. She wore a light shawl over her shoulders against the cool of the evening. Her face looked tired and drawn.

"Joseph and I have talked over your situation," Mrs. McGrew began. "We are prepared to propose something that may be the solution to your problem, at least temporarily.

"I will begin by saying that I believe the wisest thing would be for you to return to Philadelphia immediately. You have no way of knowing the hardships life in these mountains can bring on. Unfortunately, you cannot make the trip alone and there is no one here who can spare the time to take you. So let me ask you, how do you plan to survive here?"

Maggie looked down at her feet. "I don't know, ma'am."

The older woman took a deep breath. "I see. Well, harvesttime will be on us soon and we can use an extra pair of hands around here. We are prepared to offer you room and board in exchange for your labor in this household until such time as you can return to Philadelphia, which will most probably be in the spring. Is that agreeable to you?"

Maggie felt a sinking feeling. This was exactly the kind of thing she had left Philadelphia to avoid. At least in the city, she had known the people she was working for. But this woman hadn't said a kind word since she'd walked through the door. Maggie shuddered at the thought of being at her mercy. But even while she was thinking these thoughts, Maggie knew she had no other choice. At least for now, she decided, she would go the humble way.

Maggie summoned up a weak smile. "Thank you, ma'am."

Mrs. McGrew nodded.

"I want to make it clear at the outset that you are neither a guest nor a boarder in this house. Your position will be the same as a bound-out girl's would be. You may consider yourself a servant, to put it in plain terms.

"Your duties will be to help me in the house and garden in whatever way I deem necessary. You will answer directly to me. There is to be no complaining to my husband. He has no authority in this household. Is that clear?"

Maggie nodded.

"Then let me ask you one more question. Are you the tearful type?"

Maggie shook her head. "Not really."

"Well, if you are, we'll find out soon enough. I must also say that although Franny and I didn't always see eye to eye, she kept a clean house and minded her own business. You do the same and you'll not fare badly here. Any questions?"

Maggie shook her head.

"Very well. Go up and get a good night's rest. We begin boiling clothes right after breakfast."

"Thank you, Mrs. McGrew," Maggie said.

Maggie turned and climbed the ladder to the loft. Annie was sleeping peacefully on her straw mattress. Maggie found a blanket to roll up in. She lay there, staring at the rough boards overhead. Downstairs, she heard little Lyons cry.

She rolled over and peeked down through the slits in the board floor. Mrs. McGrew sat nursing her child by the hearthside, rocking. Maggie wondered what kind of strange, bitter woman she had bound herself out to. As she peered down at Mrs. McGrew's face, it occurred to her that, even suckling her tiny son, there was no tenderness in this woman's face, only a fierce and enduring sadness.

MAGGIE THOUGHT SHE KNEW all about hard work. But whatever she had done in her life was nothing compared to what Mrs. McGrew expected of her. Maggie soon learned that a woman's life on the frontier wasn't anything to be envied.

On Maggie's first morning, Mrs. McGrew sent the two girls out for firewood. At the edge of the millpond, Annie showed her a dead tree that had come down in a big storm.

Using their axes, the girls worked together, trimming off the dead limbs and hauling them up to the woodpile. They worked silently, sweating in the morning sun as they carried armloads of wood from the pond to the house.

The family stopped for their main meal at noon, which Mrs. McGrew had spent the morning preparing. Joseph McGrew came in and sat at the head of the table, food and drink disappearing into his mouth at an alarming rate.

When he had finished, he wiped his mouth with a cloth napkin and took a seat by the window.

"Excellent land we have here," he said to no one in particular. "Our table overflows with the bounty of this fertile soil."

Mrs. McGrew frowned. "The beans and squash don't cook themselves," she said sourly.

McGrew arose and brushed the crumbs off his vest. "Well, best be getting back to the mill. Excellent meal, Maura."

Maggie helped Mrs. McGrew clear the table. Then, glad to be in the open air, she and Annie headed for the woodpile.

By the end of the day, Maggie's hands were blistered from the axe handle and her arms and back were sore from carrying the firewood.

That night, after the evening meal, Maggie climbed the ladder to the sleeping loft and fell asleep, too tired to undress. Annie slipped the muddy shoes off Maggie's feet and tucked the blanket around her shoulders, then sat for a long time, gazing at her new companion in the dim light.

The days that followed were filled with the drudgery of frontier life: washing, cooking, mending, hauling, and chopping. It was a lot to expect from a young girl. But Maggie noticed that Mrs. McGrew expected no less from herself. Mrs. McGrew went about the dreary tasks slowly, methodically, without a cheerful word or a smile, as though she was carrying some great burden.

Annie was there to brighten the dark sadness that Mrs. McGrew cast across their lives. Maggie and Annie grew to be like sisters. Once a week Mrs. McGrew allowed Maggie to go up to Franny's cabin to bake up bread for the week. On those days the girls felt free as birds and light as air. Sometimes, when Mrs. McGrew couldn't spare Annie, Maggie went to the cabin alone. At these times Maggie felt Franny's presence strongly in the cabin. The solitude gave her the strength to go on.

Jake stopped by the cabin one day while Maggie was baking.

"Found yerself a home, have you, girl?" he asked.

Maggie nodded. "I'll be staying around until the spring anyway, bound out to the McGrews."

"I figgered as much," Jake said. "And suits me fine so long's I kin get a taste of bread every now and again."

Maggie was glad to give him a loaf to carry away

55

in his shoulder bag. Mrs. McGrew would never know and Maggie enjoyed seeing the old man, even if he was supposed to be dangerous.

The mill was especially busy that fall. Farmers in the valley grew corn and rye and brought their crops to the mill to be ground into cornmeal and rye flour. Since there was no coin money to be had, McGrew simply kept a portion of the grain in payment. He even set up a credit system that allowed him to be both businessman and politician, something he greatly valued. McGrew sought everyone's friendship. In most cases, he got what he wanted. He was an irrepressible character who was as full of jokes as his wife was somber.

One day the McWilliams family from downstream came by to unload a wagonful of corn. The two families had the noon meal together while they were waiting for the corn to be ground. Maggie served her bread.

Mrs. McWilliams and Maggie were helping Mrs. McGrew do the washing when the neighbor woman complimented Maggie on her bread.

"You Callahan women certainly can bake," she was saying. "I wish I could do the same. But I just don't have the time. A bread like that would surely brighten up our meals."

"Well," Maggie offered, "if you like, I could bake up a few extra loaves for you. I go up to Franny's to bake every Saturday, and it would be no trouble to do a few more loaves this week. You could come by the mill and pick them up Sunday."

Mrs. McGrew, working nearby, stiffened.

Mrs. McWilliams beamed. "That would be wonderful, Maggie. Of course, I'd want to give you something for your trouble."

Maggie thought for a moment. "Well, you were saying that you dipped tallow candles last week; we could surely use some of those."

"Hold it," Mrs. McGrew said. "Don't be so free with that bread, Maggie. Remember that you are in my employ and that the fruits of your labor belong to me."

Maggie set her anger aside and nodded. "I know that, Mrs. McGrew. But, like I said, it's no extra trouble for me and we do need the candles. Think of the work it would save us."

Mrs. McGrew nodded. "I'm not contesting that, Maggie. But this should be my decision, not yours. I have no objection to this bread trading so long as it doesn't interfere with your other duties and so long as you trade for things we really need, no foolishness."

"Of course," Maggie said.

Mrs. McGrew cast a freezing glance at Mrs. McWilliams, then picked up a bucket and went out the door toward the pond.

"I can't understand why she's so rude," Mrs. McWilliams said after the other woman had gone. "If you were in my household, I'd treat you different, sure. I declare, Maura McGrew is the sourest woman I know."

Maggie hung her head.

Mrs. McWilliams touched Maggie's hand and whispered, "You know, she wasn't always that way. When Maura and Joseph first came to this valley, they were the gayest couple you could ever wish to meet. But it's five years now that Sarah's in the grave, and Maura still walks around like a woman in mourning."

Maggie asked, "Who was Sarah?"

There was a moment of uncomfortable silence. Then Mrs. McWilliams brushed it aside.

"Don't mind me, Maggie. Just foolish woman's talk is all. I've said too much already." Then she changed the subject.

Although she never asked anyone else about it, scarcely a day passed when Maggie didn't wonder about Sarah. She noticed the McGrews rarely talked about their early days in the valley, and Maggie came to sense that there was some dark secret hidden there.

When the news of Mrs. McWilliams' deal with Maggie spread, other women followed suit. Soon Maggie was baking twenty loaves a week for the neighboring families. The things the family got through trade—fresh meat, soap, cloth, and tools—made their lives easier, and so long as Maggie could do her bread baking in one day, Mrs. McGrew didn't object.

One day that fall Joseph McGrew got a letter from his sister Catherine in Lancaster. She proposed that she send her nineteen-year-old son, John, out to apprentice to McGrew at the mill. Always eager for an extra hand, McGrew agreed.

It was on an overcast afternoon in early September that the packtrain carrying McGrew's nephew arrived in the valley. McGrew took the whole family in the wagon down to the fork of the trail at General Potter's house to meet John.

McGrew's mill and Potter's house were the two most important spots in that end of the valley. The mill was the center for business and Potter's house served as a combination fort and meeting place. In case of Indian trouble, the settlers had agreed to make a stand at Potter's fortified house. But Indians had made no trouble in years. For the most part, people were drawn to Potter's because it was located on a main trail and because Potter was an influential, energetic man who knew how to get things done.

When McGrew pulled the wagon up before the house, they could see two freshly killed deer hanging from their hind legs on a tripod before the house.

"Looks like Potter's rifle has been true again," he said. "Maura, a taste of venison would be good this time of year. I believe I'll arrange a trade."

"Very well," Mrs. McGrew said. "But don't barter our lives away for it."

Just then John came striding out through the front door. He was handsome, and from the way he walked, Maggie could tell that he knew it. McGrew got down from the wagon and went over to shake his hand.

"Good to see you, my boy. You've grown tall since I've seen you last, eh? Come and say hello to the family—we have a new child, Lyons."

They walked toward the wagon. John's eyes instantly fell on Maggie.

"This is our hired girl, Maggie Callahan," McGrew said.

John reached up to where Maggie sat in the back of the wagon and took her hand.

"Just as pretty as Uncle Joseph told me you'd be," he said. "I'm sure we'll be seeing a lot of each other." Then he winked.

Maggie drew her hand back. She took an instant dislike to this brash stranger.

Potter, a short powerful man, came through the doorway and motioned the men inside. "Have a drink before you leave, gentlemen?"

McGrew smiled. "Come along, my boy, you're

about to get your first lesson in commerce on the frontier."

The men disappeared inside. Twenty minutes passed.

"Never did see them do any business without a jug of whiskey to wash the deal down," Mrs. McGrew said testily.

At that moment McGrew came through the open doorway, tripped over the doorsill, and fell flat on his face. John stumbled out after him. He bent over the older man.

"Uncle Joseph, are you alright?" he asked.

McGrew scrambled to his feet.

"Of course, John. Must be those benches we were sitting on. Cuts off the blood flow to the legs, makes a man's knees go wobbly."

Potter had taken off his coat and rolled up his sleeves. "Let's get that deer loaded up," he said. "Storm's on the way, I can feel it in my bones."

With some grunting and cursing, the men managed to load the deer into the wagon. John climbed up into the wagon bed, pulled an old blanket over his head, and was instantly snoring loudly. McGrew walked around and, after several tries, managed to vault himself up into the seat.

"Joseph McGrew," Mrs. McGrew said sternly, "you're drunk as a skunk."

McGrew drew himself up into the picture of

mock dignity. "Maura," he said, "you cut me to the quick. I was merely—"

"I know exactly what you were doing." She glanced overhead. "If we hurry we'll make it home before the rain hits. Are you able to handle the wagon?"

"Of course, my dear." McGrew snapped the reins and they were off, headed down the rutted wagon road toward Sinking Creek.

They had been traveling for less than ten minutes when McGrew fell asleep with the reins in his hands. He toppled backward into the wagon bed and landed beside John and the body of the deer.

Mrs. McGrew made a desperate grab for the reins and managed to snatch them up before they fell under the wagon. She held little Lyons in the crook of her arm as she turned around in the wagon seat.

"Maggie," she said sharply, "come up here and hold Lyons."

Maggie crawled into the seat and took the baby in her arms. A light, freezing rain began to fall. Maggie covered the baby's face with a blanket. She looked back over her shoulder and saw Annie moving around in the back of the wagon, unfolding an old blanket and using it to cover her father and her cousin against the rain.

Mrs. McGrew snapped the reins, and they were moving again. The rain began to fall harder now, pelting them with stinging, cold drops. Maggie glanced up at the sky, water streaming down her face. The clouds looked gray and foreboding. Suddenly, a bolt of lightning cracked overhead. Thunder rolled like drums.

Maggie noticed that Annie had crawled forward in the wagon, coming up behind Mrs. McGrew. Annie started tugging on her mother's cloak. Annie's eyes were wide with terror. She began sobbing hysterically. Her mouth moved, but no sound came out.

Maggie glanced over at Mrs. McGrew and saw something she would never forget. Etched in the older woman's face were the same lines of fear. Seeing Mrs. McGrew display any emotion would have been unusual, but Maggie wasn't prepared to see her trembling in terror. She knew something must be deeply wrong, something she couldn't understand. Surely there was more to this woman's terror than a simple lightning storm.

Annie grew so insistent in her pleading that Mrs. McGrew had to pull the wagon to a stop. She swung around, grabbed Annie by the shoulders and shook her violently.

"Stop that crying!" Mrs. McGrew shouted against the rain. Her voice was high and hysterical. "Don't you see? You're only making it worse. It won't be like last time! Annie," she shouted, "do you hear me?" Then the older woman caught herself. "No," she wailed bitterly, "of course you don't." She flung the girl back into the bed of the wagon. Annie fell sobbing beside her father.

Maggie turned to say something to Mrs. McGrew to calm her down, but it was too late. The older woman had snapped the reins and started the horses down the muddy road at a brisk trot. The road was full of ruts and gully washes, and the wagon bounced so hard that Maggie had to brace her feet and hold on to the seat with one hand to keep from being tossed out.

Maggie couldn't understand why Mrs. McGrew was driving so fast. What was her hurry? A horse could slip and break a leg on a wet road like this.

Up ahead Maggie could see the place where the road forded Sinking Creek. This was normally an easy crossing through shallow water. But the pelting rain had swelled the creek into a muddy, raging torrent, nearly as deep as the wagon bed.

Mrs. McGrew saw the water too. She braced her feet and pulled back on the reins, bringing the speeding horses to a stop. Maggie thought that Mrs. McGrew would back the team up, turn around, and return to Potter's now. But she didn't do that. She just sat with the reins in her hands, her eyes fixed on the swirling waters like a woman in a trance. The roar of the water filled their ears.

A bolt of lightning fractured the sky overhead and

jolted Mrs. McGrew into action. She lashed the reins and the horses sprang forward, dashing into the creek bed.

"No!" Maggie yelled. "Don't try to run the stream!" But it was too late to stop her. The horses had already plunged into the stream, sunk in up to their withers. The rapids welled up around the wagon bed.

Maggie leaned back in the seat to keep from falling out, and as she did the left front wheel struck a rock with a jolt, tumbling little Lyons out of her arms and into the current. He was gone.

For a moment Maggie was too stunned to move. Then something inside her took over. She jumped over the side of the wagon and disappeared into the rapids. Even though the water was only waist deep, she sank in over her head and was swept a dozen yards downstream before she could find her footing and stand up. That cold plunge took her breath away, and for a moment it seemed that she might drown. But she caught her breath and began thrashing around in the water looking for the baby. It seemed hopeless.

Then she saw him, about twenty yards downstream. A dead tree had fallen into the water and Lyons' clothing had snagged on one of the branches. The baby hung, just under the surface of the water, limp as a rag doll.

Maggie let the current take her over that way and tore the baby free from the snag.

Holding Lyons to her chest, Maggie fought her way up through the shallows and onto the muddy bank. She laid him on his back in the mud and tore open his shirt, placing her ear to his bare chest. Nothing. No movement. No sound. Was he dead?

Then Maggie remembered something she had seen Franny do with a small baby years ago. She turned Lyons over with his head pointed down and gave him a sharp whack between the shoulder blades with the palm of her hand. The baby choked and vomited up water.

"That's it, Lyons," she said encouragingly. "Come on, baby, breathe!"

She continued clapping the baby's back with her hand. More water came up. Then Lyons let out a piercing wail and began to cry. Maggie was never so glad to hear a baby scream. She turned him over and looked him in the face. His eyes were squeezed shut and his mouth was wide and open, screaming for all he was worth.

"You did it, Lyons! You came back to us! You're alive!" she shouted.

Maggie glanced up the road and saw that Mrs. McGrew had made it across the river, pulled the wagon to a stop, and was running toward them.

Mrs. McGrew took the baby from Maggie, holding him tight and rocking him in the rain, wailing and sobbing. Maggie led her back to the wagon and drove the team the rest of the way home.

While Maggie put the horses in the shed, the McGrews stumbled inside and got a fire going. By the time Maggie trooped in, they were all wrapped in warm blankets, shivering by the fire.

She stripped off her cold, wet clothing and wrapped herself up by the fire. No one spoke. They just stared at the fire with their teeth chattering, as though the very sight of the flames could bring the warmth back into their bodies.

Maggie felt a hand on her shoulder. It was Mrs. McGrew's.

"Death passed close by here today," the older woman said in a trembling voice. "You drove it away, Maggie. I won't forget that."

"It was nothing special," Maggie said, shivering. "I mean, anybody would have done the same for a baby. I hope he doesn't catch a cold from this."

Mrs. McGrew didn't say anything more. She just stared into the flames.

Maggie felt a cold shiver go through her body. Death *had* passed awfully close by that day.

THE McGREWS NEVER MENTIONED anything about the night of the lightning storm again. But it was apparent
that something very elemental and very terrifying
had happened there that night, something that
Maggie only dimly understood.

Then, one day, quite accidentally, she stumbled
across the secret.

John had loaded up a mule with two barrels of
flour, then coaxed the animal up the mountain trail
to Franny's cabin. Maggie had gone along to see the
cargo safely there. Since she would be baking that
day, Maggie carried a bowl full of risen dough with
her.

"All this work I'm doing for you," John joked, "you ought to give me a cut of your bread-baking profits."

Maggie snorted. "Not much profit to speak of, John."

They were coming into the clearing now, bringing the mule around to the front door.

"How much you charge for that bread anyway?" he asked.

"I don't charge any set amount," Maggie explained. "I just trade for what I need."

John laughed. "That's no way to run a business."

"Just as well," Maggie retorted. "I'm not running a business. I'm just living."

"That's a woman's talk for you now," John said. "Haven't you got a headful of strange notions about the way the world works? Talk like that reminds me of my cousin Sarah."

Maggie's ears pricked up. She tried to make her voice sound casual. "Sarah? Who's that?"

John was unleashing the barrels from the packsaddle.

"Oh, she's long gone now. Been dead for years. But she was a spunky girl, I'll say that. She was Uncle Joseph and Aunt Maura's oldest daughter. And the apple of their eye. She'd be just about your age if she were alive now."

"How did she die?" Maggie ventured.

"Lightning," John answered.

Maggie felt a chill ripple down her spine.

"Struck by lightning?" she asked.

"Oh, sure. You never heard about this?"

Maggie shook her head.

"Well, I'm not that surprised. Everyone in the family felt pretty bad about it. It was such an unusual death and all."

"Go on," Maggie said.

"Well, funny thing about it, as nearly as I can figure, it happened right there where the road forded Sinking Creek, right at the place we stopped the other night. I guess that gave Aunt Maura an awful scare. And then, when Lyons was almost lost . . ."

"What about Sarah?" Maggie persisted.

"Oh, well, this was right after they had moved to the valley. They were all full of vim and vinegar in those days. At least that's the way their letters sounded. Then we got this letter telling about Sarah's death and after that it just seemed like their spirits were broken.

"One night they were traveling home on that road, same time of year, same kinda storm. It was while Uncle Joseph was driving the horses across the ford that a bolt of lightning came down outa the sky and struck the wagon. Sarah and Annie, who were riding in the back, got hit worst. The jolt went through Sarah's body and tossed her clean out of the wagon. Happened so fast, nobody could do anything about it. The water just swept her away before any-one knew what was happening. Uncle Joseph found her body about a mile downstream the next day.

"Annie was lucky to come out alive. As it was, the lightning burned the shoes right off her feet, scorched all the hair off her body—took three months for it to grow back. Uncle Joseph says the lightning burned the part of her brain that makes the hearing and the talking so she's deaf and mute to this day. It's a miracle that she's alive, way I see it. Wouldn't you say so, Maggie?"

"Yes, I would," Maggie said absently. Then she turned and went inside, wanting to be by herself for a while.

Maggie had hoped that hearing about Sarah would make things better. And, at first, it did. But, as the dark winter days passed, Maggie felt the sadness of the story creeping over her. Every time she looked at Annie and saw the young girl signing with her deli-cate hands, she felt the tears starting in her eyes. It was just a tragedy, that was all, and no reason for it.

Now that Maggie knew Mrs. McGrew's secret, she began to feel a strange compassion for this stern woman. Maggie remembered how it was for her when her mother died. Of course, it wasn't the same. Her mother had been sick for years and her death was almost a relief. How much worse, Maggie thought, to lose a daughter so suddenly. In the days that followed, Maggie came to see that she and Mrs. McGrew carried the same grief; they just carried it differently.

The winter was the most severe Maggie had ever known, and the gloominess she felt was deepened by its harshness. The snow piled up around the walls of the house and the wind sifted it in through the cracks between the logs, so Maggie had to sweep the floor up several times a day, brushing the snow out the front door into the wind. Even with both fireplaces going, they lived in a perpetual, bone-chilling cold. They wore their blanket coats inside and many times they sat down to the table wearing knitted mittens to keep their fingers from freezing while they ate. Hot food grew cold as soon as it was in the bowl. They used the chamber pot at night now, emptying it each morning so they wouldn't have to make nightly trips to the outhouse.

They passed a joyless Christmas. Mrs. McGrew forbade any festivities, although Maggie and Annie did exchange some knitted socks and mittens they had made for each other.

"We have no time for such frivolousness when there is so much work to be done," Mrs. McGrew had said. Actually, idleness was their greatest enemy. There was simply nothing to do. Once the meals had been prepared and the washing up was done, once wood and water had been fetched, there was nothing to do but sit in the cold and dark and wait for spring.

It was during those winter days that Maggie came to appreciate especially her weekly baking trips to the cabin. Annie sometimes went with her, and for the two of them it felt good to be up on the white snowy mountainside, away from the gloom and stillness of the house.

But Maggie loved even more the days when she went alone, walking in her homemade snowshoes up the mountainside, alive and awake to everything. She stoked her fires and kneaded her dough and baked the loaves with Franny on her mind.

It was an eerie feeling for Maggie, baking bread there in Franny's place. Many times, despite herself, she looked back over her shoulder, almost expecting Franny to be there. The voice and the feel and the spirit of Franny were in the bread and in that cabin. For Maggie it was as if every smell and sight and sound connected with the bread-baking days was a remembrance of her aunt. And she always returned to the mill with a new sense of strength and worth, pulling her fresh-baked bread wrapped in a blanket, lashed down on the toboggan she and Annie had made from split ash staves.

Sometimes, in the hours after returning from the cabin, Maggie found herself saying things to the McGrews, not out loud, but in her head. At nights, she would lie awake and compose her sentences, saying what she lacked the courage to say in her day-light hours.

One afternoon, toward the end of the long dismal winter, Maggie was baking alone at the cabin when she heard a sound at the door. When she looked up she was surprised to see Jake Logan, dressed in his winter furs and skins. His body was covered by a huge blanket coat that trailed down to his knees. He wore a fur hat made from the entire skin of a red fox with the bushy tail trailing down his back. He took off his warm bearskin mittens and set his rifle up against the cabin wall.

"Wal, girl," he said, "I seed your smoke and fig-gered I'd find you here. Roust up that fire! I'm about froze. Froze for talk and bread."

Maggie smiled. "Me too. It'll be a while before the bread's ready but I can start talking anytime."

Jake settled down by the fire. "Good enough. Start talkin'."

"No, you. Tell where you've been this winter," Maggie said.

"Wal, all right. Don't mind if I do." Jake rambled on for a good hour, telling about his solitary me-anderings around the mountains. He said that he had spent the worst part of the winter in a cave up along the west branch of the Susquehanna River.

"Jest set and look at the fire, you know. Hunt a little, let the time slide by. Spend the winter drowsy and quiet like a bear, that my idee," he had said.

When Maggie brought the bread steaming from the oven, they sat and had a simple meal.

"Durned if it ain't good to set and talk with you, Maggie. Man lives alone so much he fergits he has a voice, you know. Huntin's a quiet life, as a rule. Woods is that way, quiet most of the time—less there's somethin' unusual happenin'.

"But a man needs to use his voice every now and again. The same way he might feel for the handle of his knife in the dark, just to make sure it's still there. You know what I'm sayin', girl?"

Maggie nodded. Then she told Jake about her winter. When she finished the old man nodded.

"Even allowin' all the hardship and the downright weariness of it—ain't you still glad to be here?" he asked.

Maggie nodded. "Yes, I am," she said truthfully.

"Wal, you know, you're not a real mountain person 'til you've spent a winter up here. Most anybody kin pass a summer in these parts. But it's the ones that lives here in the winter, those are the ones who come to know the land. And I'll tell you something else, Maggie, something the people in the valley might not understand. Once you live up in these mountains and once the feel and the roll and the rills of these hills gets in your blood, you'll never be the same again. You kin travel and wander, as I have, but you'll never feel at home less'n you're near these hills. Know what I mean, Maggie?"

Maggie said she did.

"I thought so," the old man said. Then he reached into his shoulder bag and brought out a roll of thick leather. "Brought you a present," he said. "Elk hide."

He spread the hide out on the floor by the hearth. "Take off them stiff boots and come over here. Put yer stockin' foot down on this leather." Maggie did as he asked and watched as he took a charred stick of wood from the fireplace and used it to trace the outline of Maggie's foot on the leather.

"I figure you been freezin' your toes long enough in them civilized shoes. Now that yer a real mountain girl, you deserve a pair of real moccasins."

Jake cut out a one-piece pattern and sat down by the fire with a deer-antler awl and a length of thread made from the twisted strands of sinew from a deer's leg.

"This is heavily smoked elk hide," Jake said. "If you keep it greased, it'll keep the water out. You stuff the insides with a couple handfuls of deer hair and your feet'll be jist as toasty as kin be, no matter what the weather is."

Jake felt like talking.

"Used to know an old Susquehannock Indian woman, her name in English would be Small Stitches, or somethin' like that. She was given that name because, even in old age, she was skillful with an awl or needle. Why, she could sew up anything. Made me a set of buckskins once when I was a young man.

"Small Stitches said one time that you can tell an awful lot about people by just lookin' at what they wears on their feet. She pointed out that most white folks wear them heavy shoes with thick soles and high heels on 'em. Can't even feel the ground under their feet—fergit they're walkin' on the earth.

"She said that was why the white folks were so funny about land. Always wantin' to buy and sell it and trade it back and forth. Almost like they weren't part of it—like it wasn't a part of 'em in some way, you know what I'm sayin', girl?"

Maggie nodded.

"Well, that's the good thing about moccasins, you feel connected to the ground when you wear these— like a tree has roots, you see what I mean?"

Maggie smiled.

Jake slipped the finished moccasins on her feet. Maggie admired them in the firelight. They were made from one piece of leather, with a puckered toe and a seam down the center and long cuffs that could be folded up and tied around the ankle to keep the snow out.

"Thank you for this present, Jake. I thank you and my feet thank you." Then Maggie stopped short.

"But how am I going to explain where these came from when I get down to the mill tonight?"

Jake smiled. "You could tell the truth."

Maggie shook her head. "But that would place you in danger. If McGrew knew you visited me here, he might try to set a trap for you."

Jake nodded. "That's true, girl. That's true. Well, you could always tell them you took them offen a dead Indian. That would gladden their dark hearts."

Maggie frowned. "Their hearts aren't that dark."

"They're killin' off the wild things, Maggie. I don't know anything darker than that. They're chasin' the game out of the valley, fishin' out the streams, cloudin' up the skies with their chimbly smoke."

"I think you're making too much of it," she said. "After all, there are only seventeen families in this valley. There's plenty of room for everyone."

"Seventeen too many if you ask me. That's the beginning of civilization, girl. Ya know what that means to me? That means a man could get arrested and throwed in chains for doin' what comes natural. Can't think of anything that comes darker than that."

The old man smiled. "But yer doin' right girl. Keep bakin' that bread."

Maggie sighed. "The McGrews aren't bad people. It's mostly Mrs. McGrew who rubs me wrong. She's so stern and sorrowful all the time. A woman like that can drag a body down. I don't really feel like I own my own life. I'm still bound out to her."

Maggie glanced around the cabin. "Ya know, when spring comes, I think I'll give this place a real good cleaning. Maybe get some tables and chairs in here so we have something besides the ground to sit on."

The old man smiled, knowing what she was thinking. "You'll have to get the roof fixed for the spring rains," he said. "And then o'course you'll have to put in a good-sized garden."

Maggie looked at the old man. "Jake, I sometimes get the feeling that this is my real home up here, up in this cabin. Know what I mean?"

The old man nodded. "Girl, I have a feelin' that as long as you keep bakin' that bread, you'll never want for anything in this valley. You're a real mountain girl now, Maggie, free to do as you will. No need to be bound out anymore."

That afternoon, when the old man left, Maggie sent him away with two loaves of bread, one in his stomach and one in his shoulder bag.

Maggie walked back down to the mill that night, delighting in the warmth of her new moccasins. It felt good to feel the earth under her feet. By the time she reached the house, she had made her decision.

When Maggie came into the house, Mrs. McGrew's eyes instantly went to Maggie's feet. But the older woman said nothing.

It was Joseph McGrew who mentioned them when he sat down to dinner with the family that night.

"Maggie," he said, "what are those on your feet?"

Maggie took a deep breath. "Indian moccasins."

"Where did you get them?"

"I traded for them."

"Maggie, you haven't been dealing with the Indians, have you?"

Maggie said nothing.

"I will not have anyone in this house who conspires with the heathens. Do you hear?"

"Just as well," Maggie said, "because I don't plan to be a member of this household for much longer." She was surprised at how strong and firm her voice sounded. "I have decided that when the spring comes, I'm going to move up to Franny's cabin."

"Why, Maura, do you hear this? Our bound-out girl is talking of leaving us. No, child. That cannot be. After all, we have an agreement."

"That's right," Maggie said. "The agreement was that I would work for my keep here until I could return to Philadelphia. I don't see anyone anxious to have me go. And I don't have a home in Philadelphia anyway. I could make a home for myself up there on the mountainside."

McGrew laughed. "But Maggie, this is preposterous. How will you get your living?"

"I'll bake bread and trade for what I need, just as Franny did. This valley needs a proper Bread Sister again."

"But, Maggie, you're just a child."

Maggie's eyes blazed with anger. "A child couldn't work as I have in this household! Haven't I chopped and hauled and cooked and washed? Haven't I done a woman's work in this house?

"Maura," McGrew said, "speak to her, bring her to reason."

Mrs. McGrew looked across the room at Lyons' cradle. Then her eyes met Maggie's.

"Let her go," Mrs. McGrew said.

McGrew looked confused. "But Maura, don't you think this is ill-advised? We can't afford to lose her labor here and surely you don't believe this is in her best interest."

"I said, let her go. She won't starve up there, I'll wager that. And there's nothing to be gained by holdin' her."

McGrew brought his fist down on the table. "I am the head of this family!" he shouted.

"And I am the head of this household," Mrs. McGrew returned. "I said, let her go."

McGrew knew he was defeated, and his anger suddenly vanished.

"I mean you no harm, Maggie," he said amiably.

"It's not just our own self-interest I care about; I fear for your safety. We have come to grow quite fond of you here. It would grieve us deeply if you came to some harm at the hands of the savages. I beseech you. Avoid the Indians at all costs. They are not human as we are and know nothing of goodness or mercy."

McGrew suddenly became very interested in the food on his plate. "I'll be glad when the spring comes and we don't have to eat this parched corn anymore," he said.

The spring did come. And just as she had willed, Maggie moved her few possessions up to Franny's cabin and began to make herself a home.

Her first evening alone in the cabin she made herself a simple supper and ate it sitting in the open air on her doorstep.

An early moon rose up yellow and full above the mountains. It was a warm April night. Maggie decided to enjoy her new freedom by taking a moonlit walk. She walked to the edge of the clearing and found a deer path, leading her up the mountainside. She walked quietly, feeling the ground under her moccasins. There were still patches of snow in sheltered places in the woods but the wind blew warm, carrying the promise of spring. She followed the path to the top of the mountain. This was the first of the seven mountain ranges and was called First Mountain.

She gazed down at the valley below. It seemed very quiet and serene. Here and there she could see plumes of chimney smoke rising from points on the moonlit landscape.

Then she turned her face west, toward the mountains. The wind blew, kicking her red hair out in the breeze. She could feel its force pushing against her body. She looked westward, out over the seven mountain ranges and saw those ridges rolling across the horizon like dark, humpbacked snakes. She knew that somewhere out there, toward the Ohio Valley, Franny was still alive, plowing and planting and baking bread. And that thought was a tremendous comfort to her.

MAGGIE'S FIRST SUMMER in the wilderness passed like all summers in the mountains: gloriously. And quickly. The summer ended long before Maggie was ready. When the first cool days of the fall came on, it was almost as though there really hadn't been any summer at all. The whole season seemed little more than a half-remembered dream.

It was an important summer for Maggie. Settled in Franny's cabin, she didn't feel bound out anymore. She felt like she was becoming her own woman. She was the Bread Sister of Sinking Creek, just like Franny before her.

And just as they had done with her aunt, the settlement women traded for the bread and came to Maggie's door whenever they needed a warm welcome ear. There were troubles aplenty on the frontier and Maggie got to hear all of them. In that way she became a friend to women many years older than her. She gained a special trust, the kind a Bread Sister should have. Maggie began to see that there was a great deal more to being the Bread Sister than simply baking bread. It had to do with a way of giving that Maggie was only beginning to understand.

One day Mrs. McWilliams came walking up the trail with her daughters, Clara and Mary, who were a little younger than Maggie. Maggie saw them coming and hurried out into the yard to meet them.

"What's this you're carrying?" Maggie asked, taking a large bundle from Mrs. McWilliams' arms.

"Have her open it out here!" Clara shouted. "I want to see it in the daylight."

Mary laughed. "Mama finished it last night by lantern light."

Mrs. McWilliams nodded. "It's for you, Maggie, for all the bread and happiness you've brought us. Your bread has warmed us on many a cold night. I hope you'll accept this gift from us—it'll keep you warm this winter."

Maggie tugged at the cords holding the bundle and, a moment later, unfolded a large bed quilt.

Maggie's eyes widened. "This is wonderful. I don't know what to say."

"Don't say a thing," Mrs. McWilliams said. "The girls and I stuffed this with downy turkey feathers, so it'll keep you nice and warm. All you need now is a husband to go with it."

The girls laughed. Maggie shook her head. "A little early in my life for that," she said.

"Not at all, Maggie. I was married when I was your age. If I were you, I would start to look around. In case you haven't noticed, McGrew's nephew John has been looking your way."

Clara and Mary laughed hysterically. Maggie felt herself blushing.

"That's foolish talk," Maggie said quickly, trying to cover her embarrassment. "I don't need a husband. I have everything I need right here. There's fresh water from that stream over there and firewood aplenty. The cabin roof is still good and the chimney works when the wind's blowing right.

"I've got the bread and neighbors who come and trade me for what I need. With that and the garden out back, I don't want for anything."

Mrs. McWilliams smiled sadly. She placed a hand on Maggie's shoulder. "You're at a special place in life, Maggie. Hold on to it as long as you can."

Then she and her girls packed up their bread loaves and were off down the mountainside.

Maggie stood there, in the sunlit grass by the cabin door, holding the turkey feather quilt, thinking about Mrs. McWilliams' words.

"Foolish talk," she muttered to herself, then turned and went inside.

It was going to be a cold winter that year. Everybody said so. Jake even mentioned it when he visited Maggie's cabin that fall.

"The signs is clear, girl," he said. "Hairs are long on the caterpillar and squirrels are diggin' deep. Means we're in for a real mean winter, mark my words."

They talked until late. Then Jake rolled up in his woolen blanket by the fire, and Maggie retired to her rope mattress bed, wrapped warm in her turkey feather quilt. The next morning at breakfast, she said, "Jake, I had a dream about you last night."

The old man scratched his head. "Always interested in dreams, girl. Tell me about it."

Maggie wrinkled her brow, straining to remember all the details.

"I saw you walking through the woods, in a terrible deep snow, so deep you sunk in right up to your thighs. You were looking for me. I was lost but somehow I couldn't call out to you. I think I was in a deep, dark sleep.

"Then you saw a herd of deer, you raised your rifle to fire, thinking to collect us some meat, but before you could pull the trigger, something strange happened. The deer started to point with their noses, all of 'em, pointing as though they were trying to tell you something. As though they were trying to say 'She's this-away, she's this-away.'" Maggie paused.

"Well," said Jake impatiently, "what happened then?"

Maggie shook her head. "I don't know. The dream ended."

Jake scratched his head again.

"Well, now that's a puzzle," he said. "Ya know, the Indians set great store by their dreams. Now you take a fella like Old Hammerstone—he's an old Lenape holy man—why, he'd sit up all night with a dream like that. He'd smoke and ponder on it. And come morning, he would read that dream for ya, revealin' its true meanin'."

Maggie handed Jake a steaming cup of spearmint tea.

"Do you believe in reading dreams?" she asked.

The old man nodded. "Well, sure. I s'pose. Up to a point, that is. But ya know them Indians, they carry it too far. They read meanin' inta everything: rocks, trees, animals, plants, wind, and water. I even seed those old-timers set up at night, readin' inta the stars. Now that's too many for me. Me, I'll stick to hairs on the caterpillar and squirrels diggin' deep. Those are signs a body can depend on."

The old man was right about the weather. The snow started falling the day after he left and kept right on falling, thick and steady, for five days. The mountains were covered with a fresh white mantle of snow. Leafless trees stood out stark and black against the whiteness of the mountainsides. The small streams froze solid. Sinking Creek became clogged with snow and ice. Then the winds came and began pushing the snow around, piling it into drifts that, in the hollows, were as tall as a person. The wind howled for days after the snow stopped falling.

Sometimes at night, during the snowstorms, Maggie felt as though she was riding in the cabin of a sailing ship, plunging through a raging storm at sea.

But she was safe and snug. She had plenty of firewood piled by the door. She snapped off the icicles that froze to the eaves and melted them down for water. She had stored provisions—dried herbs and kegs of flour and pots of honey and strings of dried apples. She had a sense of great wealth and security.

On these snowbound days, as a special gift to the people in the valley, Maggie baked up fifty loaves of holiday breads. The dough was formed into twirls and topped with dried apples and cherries. Some loaves came out of the oven looking lopsided and funny. But others were masterpieces.

The day before Christmas, the weather grew calm and cleared. Maggie decided to bundle up the bread in a blanket and take it down to the mill to give out to the neighbors when they came by on their regular rounds. She planned to stay Christmas Eve with the McGrews, then return late on Christmas Day.

Traveling on these winter days, Maggie found that it was easiest to transport the bread on the toboggan. She and Annie had made the toboggan long and narrow so it would pass easily down the trail; it was nine feet long and a little less than a foot wide. In front, the staves were bent up into a graceful curve, like the front of a horse-drawn sleigh. Maggie lashed the bread bundle down with a long piece of rope.

As she was completing the lashings, she saw Annie toiling up the mountain trail, clomping along in her snowshoes. Like Maggie, she was dressed warmly, in a thick woolen blanket coat, layers and layers of warm stockings, thick boots, and a knitted cap and mittens.

"Merry Christmas!" Maggie shouted. Her breath made clouds in the air.

Annie took off her mittens so she could sign properly.

"Some storm," Annie signed. "It's good to be outside. Are you headed down to the house?" Maggie nodded.

"Good," Annie signed. "Because Papa sent me to fetch you. We're having a big gathering at the house tonight and Papa said you're to come and bring some bread."

"Your father thinks of everything," Maggie said. "But I thought your mother disapproved of parties."

Annie laughed. "Papa talked her into it this year. He says it's important for his political career to have everyone in the valley over for a party. He's going to make a speech."

Maggie smiled. "I wouldn't miss that for anything," she said. "I hope your mother isn't too upset by all the festivities."

"The storm helped a lot," Annie signed. "Mama got so stir-crazy from being inside that she even got out needle and thread and helped me string popcorn chains for decorations."

Maggie was hungry for sociability after her days of solitude at the cabin. "Let's go!" she shouted.

They started down the mountain trail. Annie walked ahead, breaking the trail with her snowshoes. Maggie walked behind, dragging the toboggan behind her. It slid easily over the packed snow. Because the snowshoes were so clumsy to walk in, both girls carried walking sticks to help keep their balance.

About halfway down the mountainside, well into the thick hemlocks, where the trail shot steeply downhill, Annie stopped. She turned around on the trail and removed her mittens. Maggie knew she had something to say.

Annie's hands moved gracefully through the cold air.

"This is too slow," she signed. "Let's just hop on this thing and ride down to the mill. We'd be there in no time."

Maggie had never attempted the mountain trail on the toboggan, but she saw the sense in what Annie had said. It was a fairly straight shot down to the flatlands, she reasoned. They could probably take the turns all right, and if they got going too fast, all they had to do was put out their feet and stop themselves.

Maggie made the sign for "I agree." They knelt and began unlashing the bundle so they could shift it back in the bed of the toboggan, making room for them to sit in front, directly behind the bow. They lashed down their walking sticks and snowshoes. Maggie seated herself in front and Annie pushed them off and jumped on behind, locking her arms around Maggie's waist.

It was amazing how quickly the toboggan picked up speed. The girls hurtled down the mountainside, the wind tearing at their clothes and hair.

Then it happened. Maggie didn't even see the half-buried log lying in the center of the trail. Even if she had, there wouldn't have been a way to avoid hitting it.

The bow of the toboggan glanced off the log and they went flying off the trail, careening down through the woods. They whipped through a blackberry thicket. The branches stung their faces as they flew past and kept right on going. Trees flashed by in a blur. Maggie felt Annie clinging to her waist in sheer terror.

For a moment they were headed directly for a huge hemlock tree, which would have smashed them to splinters. But somehow they managed to lean to the side and veer the toboggan away at the last moment.

Then Maggie saw it up ahead, a deep sinkhole filled with boulders and drifted snow. Before Maggie could put out her legs to stop, the toboggan shot out over the lip of the sinkhole and dropped like a rock.

It seemed as though they fell in slow motion. The toboggan dropped away from them and Maggie caught a glimpse of it flipping end over end, down into the sinkhole. The lashings came loose and the blanket flew open, scattering the bread out across the snow, all around the lip of the depression. The toboggan struck a piece of rock that jutted out from the snow and stopped dead on its side.

Maggie and Annie hit the snow, came down hard, and kept rolling. Maggie put her arms out to stop herself but then realized that the snow underneath them was sliding as well. They had created a tiny avalanche that was pushing them down farther into the hole. Annie came pinwheeling along and, quite by accident, the girls collided. Annie's heavy boot heel swung and caught Maggie on the forehead, just above the left eye. After that, Maggie passed out.

Maggie had no way of knowing how long she lay there in the deep snow. When she came to, everything was quiet and dark and still. She couldn't hear the wind. All she heard was her own breathing.

She tried to move, and was terrified to find that she couldn't. She willed her arms and legs to move. But they wouldn't. She thought they must be broken. She felt a terrible weight resting on her back, holding her, facedown, in the snow. Then a thought leaped into her mind that sent a shiver of panic through her whole body. She must be buried. Buried alive in the drifted snow at the bottom of the sinkhole!

Straining every muscle in her upper body, Maggie managed to turn her head to the side. She could tell by the feel of the snow against her face that her breath had melted a small cave around her face. As she rolled her head around, her cheek struck something fuzzy. It was her hand, covered by a frozen woolen mitten. She realized that she must have fallen with her left arm underneath her and her right hand close to her face. She worked her fingers inside the frozen mitt. They tingled painfully as the blood began to quicken in them.

She began working her hand back and forth, inching it forward like an underground animal, burrowing a hole through the snow. She moved it ahead a few inches and was eventually able to punch her way up into the cave near her face. The cave had increased in size due to her exertions. Using her right hand, she moved the snow around a little, pushing it back against the chamber walls, making the space even larger. The space was now the size of a bushel basket but only her arm and head were free.

Then she struck something hard. As she poked at it, it frightened her by wiggling. Then she realized it must be Annie's hand. Maggie thought, Annie must be terrified. Without speech or hearing, Annie's only remaining sense was the feel of Maggie's hand.

They gripped hands. At least Annie was still alive.

Maggie rested, her face lying in the snow, her breath coming in tortured gasps. It was exhausting to work in this position. Annie squeezed her friend's hand encouragingly. Even through the frozen mitten, Maggie felt Annie's friendship, urging her on.

They lay there for what seemed like hours. Then Maggie got the strength to thrash around with her right arm. She struck something in the roof of her breathing cave. She reached up and closed her mittened hand around it. It was one of their walking sticks. Somehow it had landed in the layer of snow above them.

Maggie grabbed the tip of the stick and pulled it down into the cave, then thrust it up. She felt some resistance for a few feet, then felt the top of the stick break through the surface of the snow above them.

She quickly calculated. The walking sticks were five feet long. That meant they must be buried under at least four feet of snow. All hopes of digging their way out vanished. They were trapped.

Maggie thrust the stick up at the roof of the cave. Snow poured down the hole, covering her head, but she kept thrusting, then moved the stick around and around in rings until she had made a hole about three inches across. A weak shower of light fell down through the hole, along with a draft of fresh, clean air. Now they would have air. Maggie pushed the pole up as far as she could get it and lodged it there. Then she rested, gripping Annie's hand.

She must have fallen asleep, because the next thing she knew, Annie was wringing her hand and startling her awake. They were both aware of the danger of drifting off to sleep in their situation. They both knew that that was the way people froze to death, by allowing themselves to give in to the drowsiness that is the first sign of freezing to death. Maggie had worked hard and was very tired and would drop off to sleep easily if Annie didn't remain vigilant and wring her hand whenever the grip went limp.

Maggie started to drift in and out of consciousness. At times she didn't care anymore. She just wanted to be allowed to sleep. She was furious with Annie for gripping her hand so tightly and tried to pull away, but Annie held her firmly by her mitten.

96

The anger was good because it kept her awake.

In one of her more lucid moments, Maggie began to calculate their chances. She knew they probably wouldn't be missed at the house until nightfall. If the folks at the mill came out to find them, would they be able to see the toboggan trail in the dark? And would they know where to dig even if they found the toboggan lying on its side in the sinkhole? Maggie knew that they had to be found tonight. She knew the two of them would never survive the night in the terrible, bone-chilling cold.

She was hanging on the edge of sleep as if she were hanging on the edge of a high cliff, waiting to fall, wanting to fall.

Maggie lay awake like that for hours. It grew darker. She was half awake and half asleep, waiting out the terrible cold and fighting off the almost irresistible urge to close her eyes and drift off into what she thought would be the softest and most comfortable sleep she had ever known. And then she could resist sleep no longer.

JAKE LOGAN FELT LIKE a fool for traveling in this weather. But he knew if he kept pushing, he would make Maggie's cabin by nightfall.

He felt a powerful urge to visit Maggie on this Christmas Eve. She was a link with the human world. And he cherished that link.

Just as the sun was dipping down, Jake broke out into the clearing. He smiled as he remembered how Maggie had looked that first day she had come into the valley. He had walked right up behind her that day. He wouldn't be able to do that now, he thought. Her ears had gotten sharper. And he had gotten older.

It was strange, he thought, to get old in a land he thought would always be young and full of life. He once heard an old hunter say that it was never the mountains that quit a man, it was always the other way around. He thought maybe he was beginning to understand what that old-timer had meant.

Jake opened the door and hollered inside. No answer. He crept around in the darkness. The coals in the hearth were still warm. Her snowshoes were gone. Then he remembered that she was planning to spend Christmas Eve at the mill. He had forgotten about that. Well, he thought, he'd just build up the fire and wait for her and welcome her when she returned the next day.

Jake went back outside to bring in a load of firewood. Then he saw them, a herd of white-tailed deer, picking their way down the trail. Strange for them to travel in such deep snow, he thought. They usually stayed holed up somewhere in weather like this. Jake was puzzled until he noticed that Maggie's toboggan had packed the snow into an easily traveled trail. The deer must be taking advantage of the path to forage for food, he concluded.

Seeing the deer reminded him that his meat bag was empty. And couldn't he use a taste of fresh venison hump tonight? He went back inside for his rifle, which he had left leaning against the cabin wall.

He checked his rifle in the dimming light. There was already powder and a ball in the barrel. He opened the flashpan and poured in a spot of gunpowder from his priming horn, then snapped the frizzen shut. He was ready. But he had better move fast. The light was failing.

He crept down the trail. All his senses were alive. The wind was to his face so the deer wouldn't scent him. He would follow the deer quietly, then circle around and take his shot while there was still a glimmer of light on the horizon.

The deer were stepping right in the toboggan tracks. That made the tracking easy, even in the failing light.

Jake noticed the toboggan tracks veering off the trail.

Then he saw them, herded up around the lip of the sinkhole, sniffing and pawing at the snow and pointing with their noses. He raised his rifle to shoot, centering in on a large doe poised on the edge of the snowy precipice.

Maggie's dream flashed into the old man's mind. He lowered his rifle and took another look at the deer.

She stood near the edge of the sinkhole, pointing with her nose. At her feet was a half-eaten loaf of bread. Down among the boulders and the drifted snow, he could see the other loaves. Then he saw the toboggan lying on its side in the sinkhole.

All at once, everything came together in the old

man's mind. Jake set his rifle against a tree and slid down into the sinkhole. His sudden movements spooked the deer and all of them snorted and bounded away.

Jake found the nub of the walking stick jutting up through the snow. He began digging furiously with his mittens. The first thing he saw was Maggie's head, her hair frozen to the snow. Using his mittens like twin shovels, he dug her out. Her face was blue with cold. He scraped back most of the snow but when he tried to lift her out he saw that her hand was frozen to something.

It was then that he discovered Annie's hand and realized that she was buried as well. Quickly, he swept the snow back from Annie's dark form.

All the while he was digging, his mind was working furiously, considering the things he could do. He could gather wood and strike up a fire. But that would take time and he didn't know if he could thaw them there in the open. No, he would have to get them in out of the weather.

He considered strapping them to the toboggan and pulling them up to the cabin. But that would take even longer.

Then he realized what he must do. He would have to take the girls downhill, down to the mill. It would be fast and sure and even though he knew McGrew might make trouble for him when he got there, he realized it was the girls' best chance.

Jake wrapped the girls in the blanket the bread had been in and lashed their bodies to the toboggan. He checked their breathing by placing his ear down close to their lips. They were still alive, sure enough, but Jake knew they were in that deep frozen sleep that comes before the white death.

With his rifle in one hand and the toboggan drag-rope in the other, he heaved them up out of the sinkhole and backtracked to the mountain trail. Jake skidded them downhill fast, trotting along through the deep snow to keep up. When he reached the mill, he was surprised to see that the yard was a mass of sleighs and horses. Inside he could hear the laughter and shouting of dozens of people.

He kicked the door open and dashed into the house, pulling the snow-covered toboggan right across the wooden floor and up to the blazing fire in the hearth.

The guests, seated at the table and lounging around the fire, gasped in terror. John, who had been standing near the door, moved to bar Jake's way. "What's the meaning of this?" he demanded.

Moving forward like an old bear, Jake swung one of his huge mittened hands and knocked the young man out of the way, sending him sprawling out across the floor.

The wind howled in through the open door. Jake

knelt and threw back the blanket that covered the girls' faces. They lay like two corpses, half covered with ice and snow.

Someone in the back of the room started wailing. It was Mrs. McGrew. She broke through the crowd and fell on her knees by the toboggan.

"They're dead!" she screamed. "Dead and gone!"

The old man shook his head. "No, they ain't. Now lookee here, gimme your hand." He took Mrs. McGrew's hand and placed it by Annie's lips so she could feel the shallow breathing that still ebbed and flowed within her.

Jake turned around and looked at the rest of the people. They stood wide-eyed and stunned by what they saw.

The old man's voice cracked like a whip. "No time fer standin' and starin' now! There's still a trickle o' life left in these two and we kin bring 'em back if we move smart now! Git that door closed! Some o' you men, get that fire roused up! You women bring kettles o' coldish water over here to bath 'em in! Move, now!"

People began scurrying about like ants. McGrew brought out an enormous set of bellows and began building up the fire. Some women knelt down by the girls and began to cut the frozen clothing off their bodies with bread knives and sewing scissors.

Once the girls were wrapped in warm blankets by

the fire, Jake coached the women on how to soak the girls' feet and hands in lukewarm water and warm them up slowly.

When their frostbitten toes and ears and fingers began to thaw, Maggie and Annie came out of their sleep and began howling in pain.

Maggie, wild-eyed, grabbed Jake's sleeve and drew him down to her.

"Can't you make it stop, Jake? The pain's something awful."

The old man nodded. "I know, girl, I know. Froze a couple toes in my time, that I have. But you should be glad, girl. Be glad yer alive to feel the pain."

Maggie nodded, her eyes closed. "I know, Jake, I know."

The old man chuckled. "It was yer dream. Them deer led me right to ya."

Maggie didn't understand that. And her mind was too clouded with pain for her to care. But she realized that Jake was right. She was lucky to feel the pain, she and Annie. They were lucky to be alive.

Jake stood up and glanced at the front door of the McGrews' house, bolted against the cold weather. It was a dozen steps away. If he moved quickly through the confusion, he thought, he might be able to slip out the door and make his getaway.

People had begun to celebrate now, raising their glasses and shouting, doubly merry because the girls were safe and sound. Across the room, Jake saw McGrew watching him. The big man sat down his tankard of cider and shouldered his way through the crowd. Jake prepared himself to fight his way out if need be.

McGrew stood facing the old man. "I saw you looking toward the door," McGrew said. Then he smiled broadly and extended his hand.

"I wouldn't turn a dog out on a night like this," McGrew said. "You saved my little girl's life and Maggie's too. You can't be all that much of a heathen to have done that. Stay and be our guest this evening. After all, it's Christmas."

Mrs. McGrew came and took Jake by the arm. "I've set a place for you at the table. Come and sit."

The heavy plank table was loaded with a savory feast, roast goose with wild grape sauce, sweet potatoes, corn cakes, broiled venison, and hot onion soup. It was enough to make the old man's mouth water.

People settled down and sat.

"Let us pray," McGrew said. "We are thankful," he began, "for the goodness and bounty of our lives as well as the miraculous rescue of our girls from the jaws of the white and frigid death. And Lord, we are especially blessed to have with us tonight a man, Jacob Logan, a buckskinned angel of the frontier. Guide him in your ways and help him to see the light.

In the Lord's name, Amen."

The *Amen*'s went around the table and were drowned out by the clatter of forks and tinware. All these miracles had brought on a terrific hunger.

They feasted. Then they settled into that lazy, comfortable feeling that well-fed people have when the fire burns low and it's good to sit and listen to stories by the fire.

Both men and women settled themselves, close back in the shadows. Mrs. McGrew blew out the candles so they had only the light from the fire.

The stage was set. McGrew seized the opportunity to display his oratorical skills.

"Now some people say," he began, "that this has been a cold winter."

People nodded in agreement.

"But, friends and neighbors, cold? You call this cold? I have seen some cold weather in my time that would make this winter seem like a day in July. Now you take the winter of 1771—that was a cold winter."

"How cold was it?" someone asked.

"Well, I can't tell you in scientific terms, but I will say this. One frigid morning, I was walking out to the mill, whistling as I went. But I noticed that no sound came from my lips. I looked up in the air and I can hardly describe my surprise at what I saw. It was so cold that day that those musical notes had just frozen solid in the air. Hung there like icicles.

"So I reached up and plucked them out of the air, put them in my pocket and went about my work. At the end of the day I came back in the house and laid those musical notes out on the hearth to thaw. We sat at the table and heard a little whistle escape as each one thawed.

"Well, that gave me an idea. I went out the next day and whistled all day while I stacked bags of grain at the mill. Came in that night and laid those musical notes I collected out on the hearth, laid them all out in order. And we sat there that evening and listened to what must have been about an hour of music."

Laughter filled the room. A few others told their own stories, recounting cold winters past.

Then McGrew's eyes fell on Jake, who had been sitting quietly, listening.

"Tell us, Mr. Logan," he said. "Surely you must have some talk of a cold winter. Perhaps a daring hunting exploit or possibly an account of some escape from savage Indians that might delight us."

All eyes fell on Jake. He took a long time in answering.

"Well, it's true," the old man began. "I s'pose I have seen some cold winters up in the mountains. I 'member one year I was huntin' bear over on the second ridge. Managed to roust one right out of his hibernation spot too. He was madder'n a hornet. So he starts for me, with blood in his eye."

Jake rose from his seat, hooking his arms up like the bear's, extending his fingers like sharp claws.

"So I raised my rifle and was just about to pull the trigger when I realized that I had done about the stupidest thing you can imagine."

"What was that?" someone said.

"Well," Jake answered, "I'd poured powder down the barrel and I'd primed the flashpan but I had forgotten to cram a ball down the barrel. So there I stood with an unloaded gun, bear chargin' down on me."

"What'd you do?" somebody asked.

"Well, nothin' I could do. That bear had me backed up against a rock cliff and I'll tell you, I was plenty scared. Got so scared, the sweat started ta run down my forehead.

"But it was so cold that day that those little drops o' sweat froze hard into little balls o' ice. I reached up to wipe the sweat away and I felt those ice balls and I got an idee!

"I plucked one of those ice balls off my forehead and rammed it down the barrel of my gun. Just in time too, because that bear had reared up on his hind legs and was about to pounce on me. I raised my rifle and fired. The shot went off just fine. But the heat from the exploding powder melted that ice ball and there wasn't anything but a big splatter o' water goin' through the air toward that bear.

"Fortunately, it was so cold that the water refroze

into a sharp icicle. And that icicle went in right between the bear's eyes.

"The bear's body heat was so fierce, it just melted that icicle . . . and that pore old bear died of water on the brain."

People collapsed in laughter. There was no end to the laughing. It went on like that all night. Then somebody brought out a fiddle and they cleared back the furniture and began to dance. Jake even got up and danced a reel with the widow Brown from down on Penn's Creek.

Maggie and Annie watched it all from their blankets by the fire. They felt weak and their hands and feet still pained them. But there was so much joy in the house that night, a person just couldn't let little aches and pains draw off any of the fun.

Annie touched Maggie on the shoulder. She placed a present, wrapped in paper, in the older girl's lap. "For Christmas, for you," she signed.

Maggie unwrapped it and drew out a finely made basket of woven ash splints. "Thank you, Annie. It's a real gift, sure. You're so clever with your hands." Then Maggie thought about the bread loaves strewn out across the snow.

"But I don't have anything for you," she said. "Or for anyone else here. I had made the bread all special. I made you a special loaf with your name written right in the dough."

Annie shook her head and began signing. "Don't

worry," her hands said. "You give your gift all year long. You have a talent with the bread baking."

Maggie smiled. Annie watched her lips as she spoke.

"I know a gift I can give you, Annie. Something more precious than a single loaf of bread. I'll teach you the secret to making the Callahan Bread, just as Franny taught me. You've got the heart of a Bread Sister, sure."

Annie signed. "I feel like a sister to you, Maggie. It will be more than I ever hoped for to bake the bread like you do." Then, too overcome to say more, Annie settled back into her blankets and was asleep.

Maggie saw Mrs. McGrew coming to her, through the crowd.

"Maggie," she said, "I have something to say to you and I don't know exactly how to say it."

Maggie sat quietly, and waited.

"Something broke loose in me tonight, Maggie, something that's been tight and held for years now. When Mr. Logan threw back that blanket and I saw you two lying there, I knew you were dead. I just knew it. And I realized in that moment that I loved you every bit as much as I loved my own little Annie."

She began to cry. "You see, I had another daughter once—"

Maggie put a hand on her shoulder. "I know," she said softly.

"You know about Sarah?"

Maggie nodded.

"And how she died?"

Maggie nodded again.

"Well, after she was buried, I thought I would just go on, you know, but I never could be the same. I carried that grief around like a stone on my back.

"Then you came along. From the first moment I saw you, all I could see was my Sarah standing there—she'd be just about your age, you know. And it hurt, it just twisted the knife in the wound. So it was torture to be near you. But I couldn't send you away, understand? And then you saved my little Lyons."

Maggie nodded, tears coming into her eyes.

"Tonight, when I saw you lying there, I realized that it was too late. It was too late to do anything about any of it, to tell you why I acted the way I did, because you were gone and dead. But you're not dead. . . ."

"No," Maggie laughed.

"And it's not too late. Life is hard, Maggie, but it's not as hard as I've made it. And so what if it is hard? We're alive, Maggie. We're all alive and we're together. And you know what? It's Christmas, Maggie! It's really Christmas!"

Maggie nodded and they embraced for a long moment by the fire. Then Mrs. McGrew eased Maggie down by the fire where she could sleep and pulled up her blanket.

Maggie lay back, eyes closed, feeling the warmth of the fire on her face. She smiled. Someone was playing the fiddle, soft. Just before she drifted off to sleep, she heard the sound of people singing. Rising above the music was one voice—beautiful and clear like a bell, like the voice of someone who had sung on the stage. Maggie didn't have to open her eyes to know who it was.

I N THE WINTER DAYS that followed, Maggie kept her promise to Annie. She taught Annie the bread-baking secrets just as Franny had taught her, years ago in Philadelphia. Even though Annie wasn't a real Callahan, she took to the bread baking just fine. She was soon able to bake up rounded golden loaves on her own, using the spook yeast from Maggie's pouch.

It occurred to Maggie that in passing on the mysteries of the bread baking, she had become a link in a long, loving chain of women who had passed the bread baking along, year after year, keeping the spook yeast going.

Spring came on. Down in the marshlands along Sinking Creek, Maggie could see the vivid green shoots of the skunk cabbage pushing their way up through the snow that still lay on the ground. She knew the long weary winter was over.

On a warm April evening, Maggie had taken a pack basket of loaves down to the McGrews. She stayed for supper.

After the washing up was done, Maggie shouldered her empty pack basket and started for home by the moonlight. The moon had risen up full above the mountains, bathing everything in a ghostly, dreamy light.

When Maggie came to the millpond, she saw the moon reflected in the water. She was so pulled by its beauty that she sat down in the tall grass by the side of the pond to admire it. She saw the moon above, hanging white and lovely in the sky. And the moon below, reflected on the rippled surface of the pond.

"Two moons," she said to herself. She liked the sound of the words so she said them again, out loud, "Two moons."

Then she heard a noise behind her. Someone was walking through the tall grass towards her. She turned and could make out John, coming across the clearing, walking lazily with his hands in his pockets. The moonlight picked up the white of his shirt and the dark bars of the suspenders that held up his pants.

He walked up beside her.

"Mind if I set with you?" he asked.

Maggie sat with her back straight.

"It's a free country," Maggie said. "Set where ya will."

"All right, don't mind if I do."

He had scarcely settled himself before he started talking.

"You know, Maggie, sometimes I come out here and set just like this—just set and look at that ol' moon hangin' up there in the sky. Sure is pretty, don't you think?"

Maggie turned her face up to the moon. "Surely is," she said.

"And I look out across this ground," John continued. "Pretty piece of ground, wouldn't you say?"

Maggie nodded. "Yes, I would."

John forged ahead. "Now you take that rise over there, just before you get to the edge of the clearing. I've often said to myself that would make a good spot for a house, good place for a young couple to settle and get a start in life. Don't you think so, Maggie?"

Maggie looked the ground over. "Well," she said at last, "I suppose it would be all right. Awful close to neighbors, though."

"Well," John chuckled, "that's all in how you look at it. They wouldn't be just neighbors. They'd be family." John paused a moment to let the suggestion sink in. "That is, if your name happened to be McGrew. Do you catch my drift, Maggie?"

"No, I don't." she said.

"Well, let me put it to you just as plain as I can. What I'm talking about is marriage. Look, Maggie, let's quit beating about the bush. It's been on my mind and I know it's been on your mind and, well, everybody's talking about it. Everybody knows that marriage is the next step for me and you."

Maggie's eyes flashed with anger. "You? Why, I'd no more marry you than the man in the moon. And even if I did want to get married, we're not even the same age. You're way too old for me."

John laughed. "No, Maggie, not at all. I'm only three years ahead of you and besides, it's natural that the man should be older."

"What's natural about that?"

"Well, I don't know. Just makes sense, I guess. I suppose the Lord made it that way so that wives could ask their husband's advice when they get confused about something."

"Advice?" Maggie laughed. "John, I don't mean to hurt your feelings, but you don't even have the sense to lead a church meeting in silent prayer, let alone give advice. You'd do best to stick to your millwork."

Undaunted, John continued his reasoning. "Now listen, Maggie, you can't stay up on that mountainside forever. Time'll come when you'll come down into the valley and start a family and take your place in the community."

"I've got a place," Maggie said, standing up. "And this conversation is getting ridiculous. I'm headed home." She reached down for her packbasket.

John took her by the shoulders and spun her around to face him.

"You're a good girl now, Maggie. You'll see the sense of it. You'll come around to my way of thinking. Especially after this—" and he drew her to him, his lips searching for hers in the moonlight.

Maggie felt a powerful rage boiling up inside her. She grabbed him by the suspenders, swung him around three times and let him fly. John took two dizzy steps backward and fell into the millpond. A moment later, he surfaced, sputtering and hollering at the top of his lungs.

"Maggie!" he shouted. "Git me out of here. I can't swim!" He thrashed about like a drowning man.

Maggie threw her head back and laughed. "I should've guessed that," she said. She felt around on the ground and found a fallen branch. Wading a few steps into the pond, she extended the branch to him and pulled him up on shore. He lay on his side in the moonlight, coughing and gasping for air.

McGrew, who had been watching the whole thing from the house, came rushing up. He bent over his nephew.

"John, my boy. Are you all right? Here, Maggie—good God, girl, stop that laughing and help me get him on his feet." When they got him standing, John pitched forward and vomited into the weeds.

"Just swallowed some of the pond," McGrew said encouragingly. "Nothing to worry about, happens to the best of us. Now get on back to the house, my boy. Get into some dry clothes, you'll catch a chill out here."

John nodded dumbly and started for the house, coughing and shaking himself like a wet dog.

McGrew stood quietly, the tips of his fingers together.

"Maggie," he said at last, "sit down. We need to have a talk."

Maggie looked away. "Too mad to sit," she said.

"Very well. Stand, then. We'll talk anyway. I gather . . ." McGrew took a moment in choosing his words. "I gather John's proposal didn't set well with you."

Maggie turned to the older man, scarcely able to believe her ears. "You mean you knew about this fool idea?"

McGrew cleared his throat. "Well, surely. This is a family matter, of course. John and I discussed this at great length before he came to you."

Maggie moved restlessly away, barely able to control her anger.

"Maggie, I will ask you to indulge me for a few minutes more. You see, there are a number of advantages to this marriage, advantages that will benefit us all. If John listens to me, he will be a rich and influential man someday. The name of McGrew will be as good as gold in this region. All my holdings will go to him—and you, if you'll be his wife. I've come to think of you as a daughter and I see no reason why we shouldn't make it official in the eyes of God, if you know what I mean."

"I don't think God had much to do with this," Maggie said.

"Ah, now, child. That is where you are wrong. It is almost as though all this was preordained. All the pieces fit so perfectly. Take your bread-baking business, for instance."

"It's not a business," Maggie interrupted. "It's a calling."

"Now that is where you are wrong. It is a business, and a very fine one at that. Although it could be a much better one if it were managed properly.

"With your bread-baking operation located here on the premises, it would be a tidy addition to the millwork we already do. John and I would handle the marketing of your work and all you would have to do is concern yourself with the baking you do so well. No need to worry yourself about the business end of things."

"It's not a business," Maggie repeated.

"Well, I won't dwell on this subject any longer. Think on it. But I'll warn you. I wouldn't take too long in making up my mind. I daresay John is the most eligible bachelor in the valley, and another girl just may catch his eye. After all, a girl on the frontier doesn't have many chances at marriage. She'd be wise to make the best of her circumstances. Will you think about what I've said, Maggie?"

She said nothing.

"Well, then, I'll be saying good night. You think on what I've said." Then he was gone.

Maggie reached down for her pack basket. "Foolish talk," she muttered, not sure who she was talking to.

The next morning, John officially began his courtship of Maggie Callahan. He showed up at the cabin just after breakfast, pulling along a mule, loaded with flour barrels from the mill.

"Good morning," he sang out when Maggie came to the doorway. "Uncle Joseph said it's time we bring you another load of flour. Where do you want it?"

Maggie heaved a deep breath. "Bring it inside, John."

John got the barrels stowed away safely in the corner and dusted off his hands.

"You sure do need a man around here," he was saying. "Why, there's many a chore around here either too hard or dangerous for a woman to do. I have a little time before I need to be back. Is there any little thing I can do for you around here?"

Maggie thought she might give him something simple to keep him out of her hair.

"There's a woodpile out behind the house," she said. "You could split up some kindling for me."

John rolled up his sleeves and took her long-handled axe down from the shelf where it lay. He glanced once at the keen edge she had put on it, then disappeared out the doorway.

Maggie turned back to the bread dough she had been kneading. A moment later she heard a piercing yell. She dashed out the doorway and around to the woodpile. John lay on the ground, his face as white as a sheet. The axe lay in the grass beside him. Blood was seeping from a gash in his boot where the axe blade had slashed through the leather and into his foot.

Maggie knelt down and eased the boot off his foot. "Lie back," Maggie instructed. "Don't look at it, for God's sake." Even though there was a lot of blood, Maggie could see that John still had all his toes.

"You just slashed your foot along the side, you fool," she said.

John groaned.

"Oh, quit carrying on like you cut your foot off," she said impatiently.

She used his sock to mop up most of the blood, then stepped into the meadow and carefully lifted a spider's web up off an arching grass stem. She laid the filmy web over the cut.

"What are you doing?" John asked in horror.

"Spider's web will help the blood clot up," Maggie answered. "It'll stop the bleeding quickly." She wrapped up the wound as she spoke.

"I have a peck of things to do today," she went on. "You'll have to ride the mule down to the mill by yourself. Don't walk on that foot. It'll just start the bleeding up again."

She went and got the tethered mule and brought it over and got John situated on the animal's back. John looked awfully pale. He clung to the pack-saddle, his teeth gritted in pain.

"Give my regards to the family," Maggie said. Then she slapped the mule on the rump and watched it plod off down the trail.

Maggie turned and picked up the bloody axe. She noticed that the axe handle was split. She sighed. She would have to whittle a new one now. And with so much to do today.

She looked down the trail after John.

"You know, Maggie," she said to herself, "taking care of a man like that would be a full-time job in itself." Then she went to wash his blood from her hands so she could get to the baking.

When Maggie next went to the mill, she saw that John's foot was healing well although he still limped a little.

"Too bad about John's foot," Maggie said to Mrs. McGrew when they were alone, working together in the kitchen.

"I wouldn't worry about him," the older woman snorted. "He's milking that injury for all it's worth. He's gotten out of a week's work at the mill already."

Maggie took a deep breath. "John asked me to move down off the mountain and take up here on this property as his wife."

"I know," Mrs. McGrew said.

"Well, what do you say about it?"

"Marriage is one of the necessities of life, Maggie. It's a woman's entrance fee to adult life. Sometimes it's a high price to pay, but I don't know another way to do it." Then Mrs. McGrew shook her head. "No, listen, Maggie, I don't want to make it sound all bad. Life is too hard to go it alone. Don't pull a single harness all your life, that's what I say. It may not seem on the outside that Joseph and I have an ideal marriage, but it works well enough.

"As far as I can tell, when it comes to marriage, men are pretty much the same—they are all equally unsatisfactory. But since marriage is what we must do, seems to me the trick is to pick one who is the best provider and who has the good sense to leave you the run of the house and leave you be the balance of your waking hours."

Mrs. McGrew wagged a finger at Maggie. "Establish your territory and defend it. Oh, you can give them the trappings of power, the looks of it. But you know, Maggie, the real power in the community is the power of the family, and that is the woman's domain. Without the women to hold the family together, none of the sweating and grunting these men do would mean anything. Remember that, Maggie, and you'll have a better marriage than most. That's all I'll say to you, Maggie, knowing that you'll do what you want anyway."

The older woman's words had a chilling effect on Maggie. She felt as though she were offering herself up as a great sacrifice for some unknown cause. When she returned to the cabin that night, her feet naturally guided her up the deer trail, to the mountaintop where she had stood so many times.

She looked out across the peaceful valley, then turned her gaze, as she always did, to the west. And, as always, her thoughts turned to Franny. Her heart reached for Franny out across the miles of wilderness and she wished her aunt was back in the valley. "What would Franny say about all this?" Maggie asked herself. Then, an instant later, she knew. She knew what she would say: "Look past your nose, Maggie, and don't be afraid of nothin'."

"Now what does that mean?" Maggie thought. "Does it mean don't be afraid to take the leap into marriage? Or does it mean don't be afraid to make your own way, husband or not?"

Looking out across the dark mountain ridges, the answer came to her.

"No," she said to herself. "I won't do it. As long as I have a place of my own and can stand on my own two feet, I won't give myself up to a man I don't want, even if his name is McGrew."

She turned and went down the mountainside and climbed into bed, feeling settled and resolute. Maggie had no way of knowing this would be the last night she would spend in the cabin she loved so well.

JOHN'S FOOT SEEMED TO be healed enough the very next day for him to make his way up to the cabin and resume his courting of Maggie.

They had been talking for only a few moments when John laid a hand on Maggie's shoulder.

Her voice took on a hard edge. "John," she said, "I don't have a millpond to pitch you in up here but I won't hesitate to bark your shins if you lay a hand on me again."

John drew his hand back and responded with his usual good humor. "You'll come around to it, Maggie. All women do eventually."

Then he changed the subject. "What can I do for you today? There must be a mess of things that need to be done around here with me laid up for so long."

"Only women's work," Maggie said. "I'm boiling up clothes and blankets and washrags today."

"I'll lend a hand just the same," John said.

Maggie sighed. She had known mosquitoes like this man. They were troublesome, but hardly worth bothering about.

"Oh, all right," she said, "get that big kettle and bring it out into the meadow. There's a hanging tripod out there. I'll carry some of this fire out and get the wood started."

Maggie got the fire going before she realized that she was out of soft soap.

She put her hands on her hips.

"Now, we'll just have to haul all this gear back in and do it some other day," she said.

John glanced at the sun. "Plenty of daylight left," he said. "I'm sure Aunt Maura has some she can loan you. Why don't I stay here and watch this fire for you and you can go down and fetch back that soap."

"Well," Maggie agreed, "that would be a help. All right. Keep an eye on that fire, though. It's awful windy today and the fire could get away from you if you don't pay attention. I'll be back in an hour with that soap."

Maggie tied on her bonnet and left.

As soon as she was out of sight, John found himself a comfortable place in the shade. The late-afternoon sun was warm and full on the meadow. The smells of the crab apple blossoms filled the air. John lay back, his hands behind his head.

The wind blew through the tree branches overhead, dislodging blossoms, which rained down and fell all around him. "Nothing like being in love," he told himself. Then he closed his eyes and let the drowsiness of the afternoon take him.

When he woke, his first sensation was one of intense heat. He opened his eyes and they were instantly stung by thick smoke. Coughing, he sat up and looked around him.

The worst had happened. The wind had scattered the fire across the dead leaves. The whole clearing was on fire!

The leafy ground cover had caught first, then the tall grass. A few dead pines, still standing, had begun to burn with a menacing crackling sound.

John could see that the cabin was still untouched but that the wind was rapidly pushing an ever-widening ring of fire in that direction. A moment later, obeying his most primal instincts, John found himself running downhill, away from the flames.

Maggie heard him before she saw him. He came crashing down the trail, sounding like a herd of stampeding woods buffalo. Then Maggie saw him, racing headlong down the trail, hollering in a voice scorched raw with heat and fear. She couldn't understand a word he was saying.

"What is it?" she shouted.

John collapsed against a tree trunk beside her.

"Fire!" was all he could manage. "It's afire!"

Maggie looked up the mountainside and saw a billow of smoke rising about the treetops.

"Oh no!" she said. "Come on, you've got to go back up there with me!"

John shook his head. "Can't," he gasped. "It's too much for the two of us. We've gotta go to the mill for help."

Maggie grabbed him by the front of his shirt and shook him.

"No time for that. The whole mountainside'll be gone by then," she shouted.

She didn't wait for an answer. She began dragging him up the mountainside with her. At some point he began running along on his own. They topped the shoulder of the mountain together and dashed up onto the flat.

When Maggie saw the clearing ablaze, she couldn't help but exclaim, "Good God! It's afire!"

And it was. The underbrush had been burned black for a hundred feet on the upwind side of the fire. But it hadn't reached the cabin yet.

"There's nothing we can do," John shouted.

"Even if we had enough buckets, we could never carry enough water from the stream—"

"No!" Maggie said, her eyes ablaze. "You don't fight a fire like this with buckets."

She reached down and picked up two sturdy branches lying at her feet. "We can use these. Are you with me?"

John nodded. "All right. Where do we start?"

Maggie glanced around. "I figure we can let it burn over there on the eastern side of the clearing. The stream's over there and it'll just get to the stream and burn itself out. I think what we got to do is scrape ourselves a path clean across the clearing in between the fire and the cabin. We can start here and take it all the way over to the banks of the stream."

"Just rake back the leaves and brush, right?" John asked.

"Sure, anything that burns. Let's get moving! I'll start here. You begin over at the stream. We'll work our way in and meet in the middle."

John nodded and dashed across the clearing, keeping ahead of the flames.

Maggie moved as fast as she could, clearing herself a path. She had to run ahead of the flames, working in the intense heat and smoke, coughing and wiping her eyes to see.

She worked furiously, her breath coming in choking sobs. The wind gusted, blowing the flames right up to where she worked. Then she saw John, his long arms flying, working up close to her. They were almost there! They had made it! The path was almost complete. The heat was nearly unbearable now. Some of the flames caught on the edge of Maggie's billowing skirt. She tried to beat them out with her hands but the wind just blew them higher. Suddenly she was surrounded by flames. She was on fire! Seized by a terrible panic, Maggie dropped her stick and began running across the clearing, thinking she could outrun the flames. But her running just fanned the flames higher.

John saw what was happening. He acted instantly. It took him a few moments to catch her because she was running so fast. He tackled her and rolled her on the ground, smacking out the flames with his hands. He tore off his shirt and used it to smother the flames on her dress.

Maggie lay dazed in the dirt, her dress still smoking.

"Maggie?" John's voice was urgent.

She rose up on an elbow. "I'm all right. Where's the fire now?" She shielded her eyes with her hands and looked. The fire to the east was burning fiercely toward the stream. She knew she'd have to let that end of the clearing go. But the fire headed toward the cabin had stopped. Her idea had worked!

"We did it!" Maggie shouted. "We stopped the

fire!" She put her arms around John's neck and hugged him.

"Lie back now, Maggie. You should see how badly burned you are. Stay right here. I'll get down to the mill just as fast as I can and get help up here. You lie quiet," John said.

He got to his feet and dashed off across the smoking field, running in smooth, long-legged strides.

Maggie laid her face down on the charred earth. She looked down at her body, then forced herself to look away when she saw the blackened skin and places where the clothing stuck to her flesh. But, she thought, the cabin was safe. That was the most important thing.

Then an incredible thing happened. The wind gusted strong across the clearing and the fire, like an advancing army, jumped the fire lane and roared to life in the tall grass around the cabin!

Somehow Maggie managed to pull herself to her feet. She had no choice now. She was alone. And she knew she was going to have to build another fire lane now, closer in to the cabin, like a moat around a castle.

She stumbled through the smoke and flames and found herself a branch to use as a tool. Then she began the exhausting, frenetic work of clearing a new fire lane. She would make this one wider, she told herself, so wide that no windblown flames could jump it.

She worked furiously. But she was not fast enough. The woodpile caught first. The thin kindling she had split and stacked went up like matches.

Then the hemlock-bark roof caught. Maggie tried to beat the flames back but it was no use. She was surrounded on all sides by fire, backed up against the log wall. Her clothing began to catch. She knew then that she couldn't save Franny's cabin. It would be all she could do to save herself.

Maggie bent low and leaped through a wall of flame, running on sheer instinct, slapping out her burning clothes as she ran.

She stumbled out across the desolate burned-over ground until she came to the stream. She fell headlong into the shallow water and lay there, rolling in the wet mud. She soaked her dress in water and used it to cover her eyes and mouth and nose so she would not breathe the hot smoky air. The trees overhead burned and dropped flaming branches down in the water all around her. She lay there for hours, listening to the mountainside burn. Somewhere in the middle of the heat and the smoke and the flames, she lost consciousness.

It was just before dark when John led the McGrews and a group of neighbors up to the site of the fire. The men stumbled around in the poor light, calling Maggie's name. There was no answer.

"We gotta find her," he begged.

John was horrified to see that the cabin had burned. The marks on the ground told the story.

"I left her right over here," John said, pointing.

"Easy, boy," McGrew said. Then, when the young man was out of earshot, McGrew said to one of the other men, "I just hope to God Maggie didn't go back into the cabin."

They knew there was nothing to be done in the dark. Coaxing John away, the party left and headed back down to the mill, resolved to continue the search at first light.

It was the early morning light that woke Maggie. That and the chill from lying in the streambed all night. Summoning up all of her strength, Maggie dug her fingers into the mud and pulled herself up onto the bank.

In the eerie predawn light, the clearing looked like the aftermath of a terrible battle. Smoke still hung in the air. Here and there, small fires were smoldering. Everywhere, there was the blackened, charred ugliness the fire had left behind.

Then Maggie's eyes fell on the cabin and a cry escaped from her heat-cracked lips.

Nothing stood but a framework of charred timbers and Franny's stone chimney, towering above the smoking ruins.

Dazed, Maggie rose to her knees, then her feet, and walked across the clearing. She stepped through the charred doorway and into the ruins of the cabin. The floor was knee deep in ash, and the blackened timbers slanted dangerously down into the rubble.

Maggie's legs gave way under her and she found herself kneeling down by the fireplace hearth. She began to rummage aimlessly through the ashes. Her hand struck something hard. She pulled it out. It was the broken paddle of Franny's bread-baking peel. She sat in the rubble, the broken peel blade cradled in her lap, and looked up at the chimney towering over her.

"Well," she said in a cracked voice, "I always wanted a summer kitchen. Now I have one." She laughed. But the laugh got choked off halfway through and turned into an anguished cry. She bent her head and sobbed. Her tears dropped into the ashes. She knew this was the end of something.

THE SEARCH PARTY found Maggie sitting among the ashes, holding Franny's peel. They carried her down to the mill and did the best they could for her.

It was two days before she could talk. All the while John sat faithfully by her bedside, helping Mrs. McGrew and Annie with the cold compresses and fetching water by the dipper for Maggie's parched throat.

McGrew came in to see her when she seemed lucid.

"A tragedy, no other way to say it," he remarked. "You're fortunate to be alive."

Maggie nodded. "Yes" was all she said.

"But tell me, child, how did the blaze start? John will say nothing about it. It's a mystery to me."

Maggie looked over and saw John sitting nearby. His eyes searched hers, as though he were pleading with her to keep the terrible secret. She felt a sudden, almost overpowering rage toward him and she was about to speak up, tell them all what a careless fool he had been and how it had all been his fault.

Then she looked down and caught a glimpse of his swollen and bandaged hands. And she remembered that he had saved her life by beating out the flames on her body with his bare hands. Despite her anger, her heart went out to him.

She saw that the McGrews were waiting for an answer.

"Oh, it was just the wind," she said. "I had a washing fire going outside and the wind just took it. Nothing anybody could have done about it. We did all we could."

John breathed a sigh of relief and looked down at the floor between his feet.

A few days later, Maggie got a visitor. It was Jake Logan. When he came into the room, he was shocked at how pale and thin Maggie seemed, but he didn't let it show in his face. He grinned broadly.

"Good to see ya, girl," he said.

"It's all gone, Jake," she said. "All of it—Franny's

cabin, the land, the garden."

The old man shook his head sadly.

"I seed it all, girl. But no point dwellin' on what's gone. The question is, what will you do now?"

Maggie laughed sadly. "Only two choices, way I see it. I could stay on with the McGrews and be a bound-out girl again. I suppose they'd allow that. If the McGrews wouldn't take me in, I suppose someone would. I thought about rebuilding the cabin but the ground will be ruined for a few seasons and it's the busy time of year now, so there's no way we could throw a cabin up there before the fall. So that leaves one other choice. Did you hear about John's marriage proposal?"

Jake nodded. "The widda Brown fills me in on the gossip."

"Well, might be time I was married. We could have a new house here on these grounds, have my own place again."

Jake nodded. "The signs seems to point that way. McGrews ain't such bad folks. Although that young fella—what's his name?"

"John."

"Yeah, John, he'd be a real challenge as a husband, now wouldn't he?"

"I'd be marrying the family, not the man," Maggie said.

Jake nodded. "I suppose."

Then Maggie brightened. "So, what about you, Jake, just passing through or are you staying awhile?"

"Think I'll stay some. Permanent, maybe."

"What do you mean?" she asked.

"Well, you know, a man gets to be my age he gets tired of haulin' his bones all over the mountains. I believe this winter was the coldest one I ever spent up north. Man gets to feel like he should have something to call his own, you know. So the widda Brown, she's been talking about me taking up with her on her place down the creek. She's a good woman, in her own way. The signs seems to be pointing all in one direction for both of us, girl. It's taking a mate, somewheres along the way, just another part of life, you know."

Maggie nodded. "Maybe so, Jake."

After the old man left, Maggie felt very tired. She lay back and stared at the wooden beams overhead. John came in with a bucket of cool water.

"Wish that old man would stay clear of here," he said. "He gives me the creeps, he does. I brung you some water, Mag."

Maggie lifted her head a little. "Thanks." He held her head while she drank. Then she lay back again.

John sat in the chair and pulled it close to her bedside. "Maggie, you'll be up and around before long, and I think there's plans got to be made. I want

139

to take care of you, Maggie. We all do. And I want us to set up a place here on the grounds and raise kids. All right, Maggie?"

Maggie lay silent. The pain of her burns seared through her.

"All right?" he asked again.

Maggie closed her eyes. "All right," she said. She sighed. She felt very tired.

The news of the coming wedding spread like wildfire. And McGrew was sparing no expense to make it the most grandiose occasion the valley had ever seen. For him, it was more than just the marriage of a nephew. To McGrew, it symbolized a new phase in the wilderness empire he planned to build under the name of McGrew.

McGrew's enthusiasm was infectious. All the month of May and right up until the June wedding, folks in the valley cooked and sewed and readied themselves for the occasion. Mrs. McWilliams and her daughters had even made a special dress for Maggie. McGrew had arranged for a circuit-riding preacher to come into the valley especially for the ceremony.

The morning of the wedding, Maggie put on her new dress and Annie took her down to the pond to fix her hair as she had the first day they'd met.

Maggie's burns had healed well now. She felt her strength returning. She felt as though her body was tingling all over.

"Maggie McGrew . . . Maggie McGrew," she said to herself. She kept saying it over and over. It sounded to her like she was talking about someone else. Even her reflection in the millpond seemed unfamiliar.

Before Annie brushed out her hair, she sat Maggie by the water and began signing to her.

"I've got a wedding present for you. Open it now so I can see your face. I wanted it to be special." Annie laid a small package, wrapped in canvas, on the ground between them. Maggie unwrapped it and looked at the treasured gift. She held it up in the morning light. It was a deerskin pouch, like the one she carried the spook yeast in.

"Your old one looked pretty worn," Annie signed, "so I thought you might want to start your new life with a new pouch."

Maggie smiled. "It means a lot. Thanks."

Just then the girls saw someone emerge from the trees on the other side of the pond. It was Jake. He came around to their side of the water quickly.

He made the greeting sign to Annie and nodded to Maggie. He was dressed in full buckskins, complete with hunting pouch and rifle.

"You look like you're going hunting today, Jake," Maggie said.

"That I am, girl."

"Thought you were coming to see me get married off."

"Can't stay for that," he shook his head. "Gotta move."

Maggie shook her head. "What do you mean?"

"What I'm sayin', girl, is I'm afraid this is good-bye."

"But why?"

"Had a long talk last night with the widda Brown. She figured that preacher only comes through every now and then and that if he was gonna be here we oughta take this chance to get ourselves married in the eyes of God and all. And Maggie, the thing that scares me about it is that I want to do it.

"But girl, I knowed in my heart of hearts these bones still got some ramblin' left in 'em and I'm gonna light on outa here before I fergit that. The widda Brown's a good woman, but I don't know that I'd make a good husband. So I'm headed out west now. Sorry I can't stay for the weddin'. Jest wanted to come say my good-byes."

"But where will you be?" Maggie asked.

Jake nodded westward. "Somewheres out there, beyond them mountain ranges."

"That's where Franny is," Maggie said. The words came out of her mouth before she could stop them.

"Wal, yes, it is," Jake said.

"Jake, if you see her—tell her about me, will you?"

"Surely, girl, but I don't think the chances is too great—"

"Good God," Maggie exclaimed suddenly, "I wish I was going with you!"

"Now, girl, you don't mean that. This marriage thing may not be all that bad fer a young girl like you. Now you take an idee into your head like this, it could ruin a young girl's life."

"I know it, I know it," she said, "but it just doesn't sit right with me. Besides, I'm too young to get married."

Jake laughed. "So am I."

"Well, then. Will you take me with you out west so that I can find Franny?"

Jake smiled. "Girl, yer makin' a serious mistake."

Maggie smiled back. "So are you."

"Well, then," the old man said, "let's make 'er together. Franny will tan my hide when we find her and tell her about this."

Maggie laughed. "I think Franny'd do the same if she were in my shoes."

Jake nodded. "Yeah, girl, I s'pose she would. Well, we better scurry on outa here before they realize the bride is missin'."

Maggie turned to Annie. The younger girl had been reading their lips and was smiling too.

"Here, Annie. I want to give you something." She pulled her old pouch from inside her dress and pinched out half of the spook yeast, put it in the new pouch, and hung the pouch around Annie's neck.

"You'll keep the bread baking alive in this valley now, won't you?"

Annie nodded, the tears coming up in her eyes.

Maggie smiled. "You know the bread-baking secrets, Annie, and you're the Bread Sister now."

The girls embraced for a long moment there by the millpond. Maggie thought about the first day she had met the girl, almost two years before.

Then she thought of the others: the McGrews, the McWilliamses, and the other families who had stood by her. It occurred to Maggie that even John, with all of his faults, didn't deserve to be deserted without at least a good-bye.

Maggie had an inspiration. Reaching into her pocket, she drew out a white handkerchief and spread it out on a flat rock that lay at her feet. She found a stick of charred wood on the ground where a fire had been.

Using the charred end of the stick, she knelt and neatly lettered a message onto the handkerchief:

FOLKS:

YOU BEEN KIND TO ME—I DON'T MEAN ANY UNKIND-NESS—I JUST HAD TO GO.

MAGGIE

She tied the handkerchief to a nearby branch, where it was sure to be seen. It fluttered like a tiny flag in the wind.

Aloud she said, "Now, Annie, you'll have to stall them a little to give us time to get up over the mountain. Tell them you haven't seen me. That way they'll figure I just ran off and you won't be to blame, understand?"

Annie nodded. "Godspeed to you, Maggie. You, too, Jake." She made the signs with her quick hands.

"No matter what, don't tell them where I went," Maggie said.

Annie shook her head and began signing. "I won't say a word." She smiled broadly.

Jake took Maggie by the arm. "Let's move now. I think some folks are coming down this way." They ducked into the trees and were gone.

They climbed fast up the trail until they came to a place where they could stand and look out over the valley. Down below, they could see wagons, horseback riders, folks from all over, converging on the mill grounds.

Maggie could pick out the preacher in his dark coat and she could see John strutting, proud as a peacock, as people began to gather for the ceremony. And above it all, carrying up from the depths of the valley, she could hear McGrew's voice, rising theatrically above the crowd.

"Gather 'round, friends, gather 'round," he was saying, "and you will witness one of the most unforgettable spectacles this community has ever seen. . . ."

Maggie turned to Jake, "You can say that again," she said.

Then they laughed, their hearts light as birds, and turned up the mountain trail, toward Franny and the wild westward country.

THE BREAD THAT MAGGIE CALLAHAN and countless other frontier women baked was something we've come to call sourdough. Sourdough bread gets its name from the pungent yeasty smell given off by a well-aged sourdough starter, or "spook yeast," as Franny would call it.

Sourdough bread has a long and glorious history, dating back to ancient times. But this bread really came into its own on the American frontier. Pioneering families, far from the usual domestic comforts, wanted to bring along the goodness of home-baked bread.

Sourdough bread, in particular, became the choice of the frontier cook. Besides the fact that there are few things on earth equaling the downright delectability of sourdough bread, hot and fragrant from the oven, there are some practical reasons for this choice.

In order to make truly good bread, some form of leavening or rising is necessary. Leavened bread is generally more tasty and rides easier in the stomach.

Today we rise most of our breads with dry packaged yeast, a modern-day version of the ancient sourdough. But in Maggie's day packaged yeast hadn't been invented yet.

One method available was baking soda, or "sody saleratus." But many cooks frowned on its use because folk belief had it that baking soda was harmful, causing sterility in those who used it. Today we know this isn't true, but it was a common notion then. A further drawback of baking soda was that it wasn't always available in remote wilderness communities such as Sinking Creek.

That left sourdough, or "spook yeast," as the most logical choice. It was simply made. All a frontier cook needed was flour and water to whip up a sourdough starter. Sourdough was transportable, storable, durable, and cheap—tailor-made for the American frontier.

Sourdough is really nothing more than flour and water allowed to ferment in a warm place. Yeast spores from the air collect and begin to thrive in the water-flour mixture, converting the starch in the flour into sugar. The resulting fermentation creates a buildup of gases, which puff the loaf up to twice its size.

You can carry on the legacy of the Bread Sister today by baking your own sourdough bread at home.

My wife, Jacque, a magnificent sourdough cook in her own right, has tested and developed the following recipes, adapting them to modern-day kitchens.

Sourdough bakery starts with something called a "starter." This is the "sponge" or "spook yeast" that Maggie carried around her neck. It is from this starter that all sourdough loaves are born.

THE STARTER

To make the starter, place one cup of milk in a non-metal container. (A glass jar, a plastic bowl, or a ceramic crock works fine.) Allow milk to stand at room temperature for 24 hours. Stir in 1 cup flour. (White, unbleached flour is best.)

Leave uncovered in a warm place (80°F is ideal, but anywhere between 70° and 90°F is good) for two to five days, depending on how long it takes to begin souring and bubbling. Chillier temperatures slow down the growth of the yeast, while too much heat (over 110°F) kills the "yeasties" outright. If the starter starts to dry out, stir in some tepid water. Once it has a good, sour smell and is full of bubbles, it is ready to use.

Always keep about 1½ cups of starter on hand. Each time you use a portion of the starter, replenish it with equal amounts of milk and flour. Cover and store in the refrigerator. It's best if you use the spook yeast at least once a week. If you don't plan to use it for two or three weeks, it's a good idea to spoon out about half, discard it, then replenish what remains with flour and milk. If you don't plan to do any baking for several weeks, you can freeze it. Since the low temperature slows down the growth of the yeasties, allow it to stand at room temperature for 24 hours before using again.

RECIPES

Now you're ready to begin baking. Here's a simple basic recipe, adapted for modern kitchens:

Ingredients:
1 package dehydrated yeast
½ cup lukewarm water
1 teaspoon sugar or honey
1 cup sourdough starter
6 cups all-purpose unsifted flour
1 teaspoon salt

½ teaspoon baking soda

1 egg or oil for glazing (optional)

Begin with all ingredients at room temperature. In a nonmetal bowl, mix 1 package of yeast and ½ cup of lukewarm water. Stir in the sugar or honey until dissolved. Set aside for 10 minutes or until yeast becomes foamy. Add 1 cup sourdough starter.

Sift flour. Add 4 cups to yeast mixture, leaving 2 cups to be added later on. Stir in salt and baking soda. Mix with a nonmetal spoon. Turn the resulting dough into a large oiled bowl, cover it with a damp towel, and let it rise until doubled in size, about 2 hours.

Add 1 cup flour to the risen dough. Use the remaining cup to flour the kneading board. Knead well. The dough should feel elastic and satiny. Knead for about 10 minutes, until the dough can no longer absorb more flour.

Shape the loaves by forming the dough into round, plump circles. You can make one large loaf or two smaller ones. Set aside on a greased cookie sheet for the second rising. Cover with a damp towel. Let rise for two hours or until the dough doubles in size.

When the second rising is completed, use a sharp knife to score a cross on the top of each loaf. Decide which type of crust you'd prefer, tender or crusty. For tender crusts, brush the surfaces of the loaves with a beaten egg or oil. For crusty bread, place a pan filled with water in the oven with the bread, or simply brush the surface with water.

Bake at 375°F. For two loaves, bake for 50 minutes. For one, bake between 60 and 70 minutes.

The loaves are done when they turn a medium brown and sound hollow when you tap them on the underside.

Enjoy!

Once you've mastered this recipe, you might want to try a more traditional, and more difficult, one, similar to the kind Maggie and Franny might have followed.

Note: This recipe requires about 18 hours.

Ingredients:
1 cup starter
6 cups all-purpose unsifted flour
1½ cups warm water
2 teaspoons sugar, honey, or molasses
2 teaspoons salt
1 pinch baking soda
1 egg or oil for glazing (optional)

Begin with all ingredients at room temperature. In a nonmetal bowl, combine starter, flour, water, sugar (or honey or molasses), and salt. Mix with a nonmetal spoon and set aside, uncovered, for 12 hours.

After first rising, add 1 cup flour and use the remaining cup to flour the kneading board. Add baking soda and knead well. Form into loaves and let rise on a greased cookie sheet for 4 hours.

When second rising is completed, prepare the loaves for the oven and bake them in the same fashion as in the first recipe.

This recipe requires more work but you'll be rewarded with a finer bread. Enjoy it! You earned it!

Once you've become an old hand at these bread recipes, it will be a simple matter to start turning out biscuits, flapjacks, doughnuts, and cakes—all from your own perking sourdough pot.

Besides the edible results, there are more exotic uses for sourdough. They say some Alaskan prospectors used to allow the starter to ferment enough to pour off a fiery alcoholic liquid called "hootch." I tried it one time and all I can say is you'd have to spend a pretty long winter alone and be pretty downright desperate to drink that stuff. But, as a wise person once said, necessity is the mother of invention.

Folklore also provides us with other uses for sourdough. Some took a spoonful of raw starter as a bacteria-fighting medicine. Others used the remarkable stuff to chink the spaces between the logs in their cabins or plug up holes in their shoes.

Shoe and house repairs aside, sourdough is great

stuff. After you've tasted the joys of sourdough cookery, and after your kitchen has been filled with the heavenly smells of fresh-baked bread, you'll understand why Jake would say, "Bread ain't bread less'n it's rised up light and airy. Makes a man's mouth glad ta chomp inta!"